the
sharing
economy

sophie berrebi

SCRIBNER

LONDON NEW YORK SYDNEY TORONTO NEW DELHI

First published in Great Britain by Scribner,
an imprint of Simon & Schuster UK Ltd, 2023

1 3 5 7 9 10 8 6 4 2

Simon & Schuster UK Ltd
1st Floor
222 Gray's Inn Road
London WC1X 8HB

Simon & Schuster Australia, Sydney
Simon & Schuster India, New Delhi

www.simonandschuster.co.uk
www.simonandschuster.com.au
www.simonandschuster.co.in

A CIP catalogue record for this book
is available from the British Library

HB ISBN: 978-1-3985-1556-7
EBOOK ISBN: 978-1-3985-1557-4

Typeset in Palatino by M Rules
Printed and Bound in the UK using 100% Renewable
Electricity at CPI Group (UK) Ltd

To CvW

Painting relates to both art and life. Neither can be made. (I try to act in the gap between the two.)

ROBERT RAUSCHENBERG

Contents

PART ONE

PART TWO

PART ONE

1

Mirror Site

There's an art to undressing and there's an art to getting dressed again. Usually, I want my clothes to be taken off slowly. I like to have my coat unbuttoned and my skirt pulled up, to see my jumper lifted over my chest. I usually interrupt them at some point. I'd rather keep a little something on. Perhaps it is to create a sense of transience, to remind myself that I won't be staying very long; to let them know that I will soon be on my way elsewhere, that I am dropping by almost as an afterthought. I can stay for an hour, a couple at most. However long I might be there for, it is always just for a moment. Like the men who stuff their watch and keys in their shoes to ensure a smooth exit when the time comes, I have a system. Keys in the right coat pocket, watch in shoes, rings kept on fingers, and if I am in a hurry, I set a timer on my phone.

Some liked to take everything off all at once. Full nakedness upfront, achieved within seconds: 'Let's get comfortable,' they'd say. That was always far too direct for me. It reminded me of the windswept beaches of the Wadden Islands up in the north, where nobody bothers to cover up in a towel when changing, or of the relaxed half-nakedness of the locals reading the weekend papers amidst the potted palms, teal glazed tiles and art deco fittings of Sauna Deco, the little spa on the Herengracht.

The more meticulous ones would hang my coat up in their closet, and conscientiously fold my dress and belt on the back of a chair: it never ceased to amaze me, how neat and fastidious some were. A habit born out of necessity, they would say, dictated by the diminutive size of homes in this doll's house of a city. It made me smile; I certainly didn't expect such thoughtfulness. All I wanted was my bra to be tugged at, to have my tights pulled off and my knickers rubbed till they became wet.

I admit I never offered much help in the way of undressing them. Perhaps I would yank at their belt a little, or make a show of clumsily attempting to unbutton the top of their shirt. These were the most overt signs I gave out. Because of my patent indifference to the erotic potential of the male striptease, they usually took their clothes off quickly and discreetly, inwardly praying – or so I imagined when I looked at them from the corner of my eye – that they would manage to avoid the potentially comical effect of the extraction from trousers caught around the ankles.

The art of dressing up again is comparatively harder to pull off. Disappearing to the bathroom for a quick shower is one possibility. Most often, I would spring out of bed as soon as they left the room, deftly collecting the garments strewn across the floor and dressing as swiftly as possible. Falling asleep after the last orgasm was a luxury I allowed myself only rarely. I was ready to leave when they returned a few minutes later somewhat bemused by the change of situation. A dab of lipstick was a dependable way of preventing any last-minute kissing. 'Am I decent?' I would flippantly ask, all flustered cheeks, bushy hair and dreamy eyes, and then I was off onto the street, unlocking my bicycle.

At least, that's how it happened at the beginning, with men. Looking back, I wonder how much of that behaviour came out of memories of movies and novels; a bit of porn also, perhaps. I turned the first lines that Rita Hayworth speaks in *Gilda*, when she lifts up her chin, gazing at her husband and her former lover standing side by side – 'Sure, I'm decent' – into my parting banter.

It was a private joke that none of them ever picked up. But it helped me to keep up the attitude: to always act somewhat aloof and mildly interested, to not appear too voracious or enthusiastic, to learn to offset desire with modesty and playfulness with reticence. I understand better now, as I describe the subtleties of this balancing act, the performative aspect of that tightrope that a woman walks in heterosexual sex. Those unspoken rules that are supposed to make it all work smoothly.

Those rules had facilitated my early sex life in the mid-nineties in London. Now, some twenty years later, I was slowly rediscovering them, this time living in Amsterdam, no longer a carefree twenty-something but a forty-five-year-old married woman whose son had just passed his ninth birthday.

Anne Teresa De Keersmaeker, Stadsschouwburg Amsterdam, 5 February 2014

She walks calmly onto the stage. She doesn't glide, like dancers sometimes do. She wasn't already standing in position when the curtain rose. She does not march in, or prance, or strut, or shuffle. She walks casually, as if she were stepping in from the room next door. With each step she takes across the stage the slits of her black knee-length shift dress open to reveal a glimmer of pale sinewy legs. Her dark hair is tied in a low ponytail. She strides across the almost empty, uniformly black stage and stops in front of a record player that I hadn't noticed before. She lifts its arm and I hear the distinct, unpleasant scraping sound of the needle as it hits the grooves of the vinyl record when she places it on the edge of the LP. 'Once I had a sweetheart,' Joan Baez begins to sing, playing the guitar, her clear voice filling the theatre.

The woman on the stage casually kicks off her shoes and, immersed in the music, she begins to try out a few dance steps. She hardly looks up at the audience holding its breath in the dark, transfixed by this woman who now stretches out an arm, slides a leg forward and makes a little jump as she turns around. The dancer pauses and turns her head towards the record player. She wants to be absolutely sure to capture each word of Baez's 1963 concert recording. Now she turns towards the audience and resumes dancing, carried away by the voice and the words.

'We shall overcome,' sings Baez as the dancer arches her back, extends her right arm forward and twirls around, her dress fluttering about. She stretches out a leg, flexes her foot, bends an elbow. A little shuffle lifts her right shoulder. Another pause. She looks around briefly, but does not appear to see anything: mind and body entirely concentrated on each syllable of Baez's singing, on the rhythm of the music as she absorbs it into her body. She steps forward, shifts her weight from one leg to the other; her arms crossed onto her hips to form a sort of coil from which she escapes, skipping lightly, outlining a half circle with her body. She is a teenager dancing in front of her bedroom mirror. She is Joan Baez, age twenty-four, onstage at the BBC, in a knee-length floating shift, dark hair and low ponytail, playing the guitar. She is the Belgian choreographer Anne Teresa De Keersmaeker, in her fifties, dancing a solo piece on the stage of the Stadsschouwburg in Amsterdam. From one minute to the next, De Keersmaeker blends these different ages of womanhood into one: the lonely teenager in her room, the engaged young musician onstage and the seasoned dancer choreographer on tour.

2

Open Data

My unconscious sometimes speaks so loudly that things seem to come to me unexpected, unrequested but well-timed. This was early February, on a particularly frigid late afternoon, after a public reading hosted by a feminist art collective in an alternative space off Westerdok, in the newly redeveloped harbour on the west side of the city. People spilt onto the pavement talking to one another. They formed clusters that fell apart and came together again in continually changing configurations. Swaddled in coats and beanies, artists, curators, writers and others whose professional activities were as temporary and as vague as my own chattered away in the dark, forever catching up as they exhaled plumes of mist in the damp air. They were just back in town or on their way to a far-flung residence; they had an exhibition coming up, or one that was just ending, or they were working on a new exciting project they could not say much about – all still under wraps. Usually, nothing very personal ever featured in those art-world exchanges, beyond the brief mention of a partner or children. Family life was set aside; side notes to carefully self-curated creative lives that were advantageously presented to one's interlocutor. But an answer to a question I did not remember asking, to a younger woman I had never spoken with, had been voiced in quiet confidence:

'You know, Gabrielle, you should try the dating app, it could be fun, and just what you need.'

The woman's voice was Australian, and for months afterwards, I would run into her at various art events across the city, although, remarkably, I don't think we ever spoke again.

The dating app had only been introduced in the Netherlands a few months before, not long after it had launched in the United States. Weekend supplements and daily papers ran features and polls about it. It seemed they could not get enough of discussing the new rules of what they increasingly called, in English, 'dating': another example of the Americanization of Dutch culture. Magazines interviewed millennials who seemed to live with their faces buried in their phones, and asked them what they expected from it, if it was really all about hook-ups and if so, would it make relationships become more trivial. Nobody over twenty-five ever featured in those articles, which I read with the inattention of somebody who, in their forties, was clearly more the target of the publications than the app they were discussing. And yet, as much as the Australian woman could not have imagined the effect of her words, I forgot everything of the conversation that had initiated them.

•

I didn't mention anything to Anton when I joined him later at his friends Adelia and Floris's for dinner. They lived in an imposing nineteenth-century school overlooking the Da Costakade canal. The austere brown brick building had been converted into loft-like apartments, a testament to the municipality's habit of repurposing historical buildings as the demographics and the economy of the city changed. These days conversions were most often plush private developments, but this house, like many others, had long ago been a squat, legalized and then many times refurbished. Its careful maintenance now concealed that past activist history completely.

I paused before ringing the bell. I was out of breath after the cold bike ride across town, but I also needed to brace myself. Adelia and Floris were almost a decade older than me, friends from Anton's student years. They had been very hospitable when Anton had introduced his new Franco-British girlfriend into his Dutch circle of friends. Adelia was a filmmaker, these days, and Floris ran a small art foundation. They were fixtures of a Dutch art scene that prided itself on being international-minded even though it remained, under its English speaking surface, impenetrable to strangers. There would always be the occasional remark or private joke that made you realize something was out of reach. It had much to do with the politicized history of the cultural scene in Amsterdam, that went back to the 1960s and the Provo counterculture movement from which the squatters' movement of the 1980s, with its fight for social equality and culture, had emerged. That past, although it was never openly discussed, was the backbone of the art world, and you were either part of that history or you weren't. Like many foreigners attracted to the internationalism of Amsterdam, I remained an outsider. Maybe that was why it was difficult to feel at home with these people. Or perhaps it was that Floris and Adelia exuded a smugness that I found vaguely stifling.

Anton had already arrived. He leant in and gave me a long kiss and a quick neck rub, feeling the coldness of my skin. Marcus, my friend Cassie's partner, opened a bottle of organic wine while extolling its virtues and those of the wine dealer who had sold it to him.

'It's from that small place off the Overtoom, they only do organic wines.' He laid out appetizer salads and artisan breads, and described at length how the owners travelled in their small van across Italy to remote wineries in Puglia. Floris took appreciative sips before challenging him about the true merits of organic viticulture. Adelia called to Anton to serve me a drink. I took a few steps into the main room, the former school's grand hall. The elegant cosiness of their vintage rugs, mid-century Scandinavian furniture and designer lamps never failed to intimidate me.

When I walked up to the table, Marcus was explaining the reason for Cassie's absence – mentioning a delayed flight from Madrid.

'Wasn't she at the art fair over there?' I asked.

He mumbled non-committally about the fair's satellite events, and said we shouldn't wait for her; that she would join us directly from the airport. 'She is due in Schiphol around 8.30.'

Marcus followed Adelia into the kitchen, offering his services to the chef. Meanwhile, Anton and Floris began their umpteenth discussion about the effect of the government's budget cuts on the arts. I followed it with one ear, circling around them, as I looked out through the arch-shaped windows at the fuzzy orange light that bounced against the rippling murky waters of the canal.

I peered into the kitchen. Marcus was carving a chicken, chatting away with Adelia, who was spooning out the cooking juices into a bowl and piling sweet potatoes onto a serving dish. The kids came tumbling in, gangly teenagers who loaded their plates with chicken and potatoes, reluctantly sampled the salads and scarpered back to their rooms and their computer games.

We sat down to eat, enthusing about the food. I asked Floris about his work and Marcus began to tell stories about his new neighbours, an American couple who had been thrilled to discover Marcus and Cassie had connections to the United States and had wanted to socialize with them ever since.

'Problem is,' Marcus threw an ironic side glance around him, 'I find them utterly insufferable, but Cassie of course thinks we should give them a chance.'

'Speaking of American expats, I heard this story the other day,' Adelia started. 'The kids' maths teacher told me. It's about two American families, with no connections to one another, although they both live in the Oud-Zuid area, that have been destroyed by a spouse having an affair. According to her, in each case the couples didn't try to work it out, or get mediation, but immediately decided to divorce. It was over, bang, from one day to the next, no discussion.'

'And so what? It sounds very efficient to me.'

'Don't be a cynic, Marcus. Don't you think it's sad?' She looked at us. 'You know, not trying to first sort things out, to talk through problems. And then to leave these kids in the middle of the break-up, in a foreign country.'

'So, what are you saying? That they should have done couple's therapy?'

Adelia ignored Marcus' acerbic tone. She could not understand, she said, why people did that: cheated on one another and then broke up without trying to work things out. 'What is it with these young people? Do they think marriage is a walk in the park?' People had to communicate, compromize, speak together, she went on, forcefully, pointing out how 'younger people' seemed less ready to do that.

'. . . Or perhaps they have a far too idealized notion of what marriage is?' Floris interjected.

'I don't know about American expats, but I certainly have the feeling that the French expats here are very focused on the nuclear family model. They seem pretty rigid about it.' I looked at Anton. 'When we were looking into sending Victor to the French school, years ago we discovered a surprisingly conservative community that seemed to socialize around Sunday school and baptisms.'

Anton leant forward. 'French or American, or Dutch, for that matter, I think there is something going on with younger generations. People get married and they feel this social injunction to find happiness entirely within the limits of the nuclear family. So, if anything goes wrong, it just implodes.'

Adelia looked pained, toying with her fork on her empty plate. 'It must be hard to live in a foreign country when that happens; you must feel so isolated.' She looked up at Floris who was hanging on every word his wife spoke, squinting behind his round gold-rimmed glasses. 'It's so important, for a couple to function together for a long time, that each one has their own activities and friends, and of course a fulfilling career. It's just key.'

'Sure, but if these couples are breaking up over infidelity, then what they need is perhaps not to each have their yoga classes, book clubs and camping buddies, but to grant one another more sexual freedom.'

'As in?'

'Open relationships, polyamory ... all that ... why not?'

'Oh come on, Anton, that doesn't work, everybody knows that, especially a feminist like you!'

'Why is that?'

'Because that way either ends up with those pathetic old couples in swingers' clubs, or it just breaks things up anyway.' Floris smiled as he spoke, shaking his mane of brown curly hair.

Adelia sat back in her chair. 'I agree. Anton, you must know that this is what our parents tried out in the seventies, the sexual liberation. And everyone knows that ultimately, it's the men that profited from it ... And then later on they just got divorced and married their younger secretaries anyway.'

'Isn't that just a bit of a caricature, Adelia?'

'I don't know,' she replied flatly.

'Do I sound really politically incorrect,' Floris paused before continuing, 'if I say that I think it's women who don't want open relationships? That they are the ones who can't deal with them?'

Adelia, who was now offering seconds to everyone, stopped in her tracks, serving spoon in hand.

'Yes, you definitely do! Even so, I don't think open marriage is a solution.' Adelia was usually up for embracing almost any new trend that suddenly revolutionized your life. But I sensed that while politics, alternative therapies and urban regeneration were all admissible ways of expanding your existence, open relationships were maybe less so.

'Anyway,' Marcus held out his plate, 'let Floris dream on. I think it's more likely to be the men that can't deal with it. And yes, please, I would love one more sweet potato.'

'Why would that be?'

'Their egos?' I suggested. Adelia repressed a chuckle and the men remained impassive.

'But seriously, all of this pressure on the nuclear family comes from the State, the Church, it's all the work of patriarchy ... Gabrielle was telling me about it.' Anton looked at me. 'You were reading that feminist Marxist thinker, Federici, and telling me all about it the other day.'

'Yes, she is fascinating, Silvia Federici. I love the way she argues that marriage was shamelessly instrumentalized to enforce patriarchy and serve the interests of big capital. It's very convincing.'

I explained Federici's argument about the makings of

modern patriarchy materialising when the owners of the Yorkshire wool mills had raised the wages of their male workforce to encourage women to stay at home, take charge of the purse strings, have babies, and then become responsible for preventing the men from drinking themselves to death after their dehumanising work shifts.

Floris rolled his eyes. 'So that's precisely why the open relationship should be the way to go, to defy the patriarchy?'

He squinted questioningly and Anton replied: 'That's part of it, but think of those American couples Adelia was talking about; people should give each other more freedom. Sexual infidelity is unavoidable, for whatever reasons, in long monogamous relationships, so why not give the other sexual freedom, as a gesture of love, of communication maybe?'

Marcus refilled our glasses and commented on how idealistic Anton's position was. 'People get jealous, aren't you forgetting that?'

'I don't think they are jealous. Like these American couples, it's more their pride that is hurt, they feel humiliated. And that's because in the first place, they are constrained by the conventionality in which they live, like the French expats that Gabrielle knows. And then, people get hurt because secret affairs are deceitful. Lying is simply the worst thing in a relationship.'

'So, people basically are insecure, and couples don't communicate enough?' Adelia said in a neutral tone.

'Well, that's a bit of a short cut, I would say.'

'But that explains why those two American couples broke

up so swiftly, and also why it's important to talk a lot and have a fulfilling and independent life within the couple.'

I was about to argue that monogamy needed to be seriously questioned as an ideology when the doorbell rang. Floris rose and Adelia started to collect the dirty plates.

'Better late than never,' Floris announced, stepping back into the room, followed by an exhausted yet glowing Cassie who apologized for her lateness, distributing kisses and hugs, and then slumped into an armchair. Marcus walked in from the kitchen bringing her a plate of food.

•

We left, not long after Cassie's arrival, to relieve our babysitter. I headed down the narrow bike lane first, playing back some of the evening's conversation in my head. I was glad Anton had brought up the open relationship topic with his closest friends, that he was willing to open up about something we had agreed on some years back.

Anton caught up as we reached the sleepy Jacob van Lennepkade canal that extended from the centre deep into the Oud-West district and we cycled side by side along the water.

'Thanks for bringing up the open marriage thing tonight,' I said.

I vaguely discerned a half-smile in the dark, as Anton veered to avoid a car turning onto the canal.

'They didn't seem to like the idea much, though, did they? I was a bit shocked at Floris's reaction.'

'Understandable, though. I saw him looking around the

room, at his perfect domestic harmony. He wouldn't want to risk it all for a little excitement.'

'What do you mean?'

'Something happened long ago, and Adelia was not happy about it. He is in repentant mode forever. That's the dynamic between them.'

We circled around a young man who had stopped bang in the middle of the street on his bike to argue noisily over the phone, the guttural intonations of his voice resonating in the empty canal street. I had sensed a tension between Adelia and Floris. But still, I had long hoped that Anton would tell them about our open relationship at some point. To avoid gossip, if anything. 'They don't like me so much,' I pressed on. 'They would have a field day if they thought we were cheating on each other.'

'They like you, darling, it's just that they are a bit ... I don't know ... stuffy. Anyway, I love you, and I am glad we have this open thing going on and that we talk about it, a lot! I love you, Gabrielle Bloom.'

Anton extended his arm towards me and I reached out to catch his hand, leaving only one perilously steering as we cycled hand in hand further down the canal, past the city's old pathological anatomy lab that now housed a hip restaurant and art space, and turned into the Nicolaas Beetsstraat. As we entered the Vondelpark, our bikes came even closer, and we heard the muffled screech of the tyres as they reached the sandy path. The front lights of our bikes suddenly illuminated the dense rows of trees ahead of us, turning the park into a movie set.

Fiona Tan, Eye Filmmuseum, 10 February 2014

The montage of old ethnographic film footage, flickering ghosts from a vanished world, lights up the cinema-sized screen in the museum gallery. First comes an assembly of men in worn-out military uniforms and turbans standing in neat rows in a lush landscape. They seem to be waiting for a photographer to capture them in a formal portrait as the camera slowly, hypnotically, pans the group, capturing expectant and bored gazes. The scene is cut short and then four Japanese women in kimonos and obis appear, standing on a dirt path. They cautiously patter towards the camera, simultaneously playing the flute, their heads covered in bulbous woven hats that conceal their faces entirely. A sharp cut.

Now a city appears, somewhere in South Asia: the camera, presumably mounted on a car, sweeps past a row of rickshaws, their drivers standing by, waiting for clients. And then it smoothly runs through neighbourhoods filled with men and women dressed in shirts and sarongs going about their affairs. The film's motion is slowed down enough that the city seems suspended in time and space as the graceful choreography of bodies captured somewhere, sometime unfolds across the screen. Cut. Two small girls look into the camera. One gently kisses the other's cheek. Their curled hair, matt skin and clothing suggests somewhere in North Africa.

The lack of information about Fiona Tan's film forces me to read faces and movements, to project things – cultures and nationalities – and inevitably to misread signs and misunderstand gestures. More sequences follow. Somewhere in Africa: two young men and a woman, barely clothed, walk into the camera frame, pose and then spin clumsily around, moving slowly in one direction and then the other, following a sequence of steps that I can only imagine they have been coerced into performing. This is followed by shots of families and then a scene where kids in tattered clothing laugh at the camera. None of those images can erase the unsettling scene of the three men and woman forced to present themselves to the camera, and whose only possible resistance is to misperform.

The screen fades to black and when it lights up again, it shows a man in a gleaming white shirt who energetically cranks a hand-wound camera and directs it towards us viewers, grinning. As brief as his presence might be, I feel like he's observing me, putting me on the spot and under watch. I turn around. The thick carpet must have muffled the steps of the other viewers who were standing there with me minutes ago but have now left. I would have liked to see their reactions but all I can do is to follow them and walk away from the film and into the museum's foyer. The flood of light, the asymmetrical angles of the futuristic building resting on the banks of the IJ, the inner sea that separates the north of the city from the rest of Amsterdam, are disorientating after the film's dark, fragile images resurrecting a colonial past.

I walk to the pier where the ferry to Amsterdam Centraal Station awaits, eyes filled with these unknown faces, with these bodies constrained to behave and behold the camera, and these gazes telling a thousand stories, none of them directed at me.

3

Facing Forward

Towards the end of the morning the pale blue winter sky filled with clouds and lashes of rain began to blow across the city. I was sitting at the back of a tram that wound its way through the Indische Buurt neighbourhood. It departed by the waters of the Eastern Docks, and after swerving a little to the right, it began to outline a circle along one of the furthest of the concentric streets that give maps of Amsterdam their familiar clam-like shape. A week or so after the public reading on the Western Docks I had yet to take up the suggestion made by the Australian woman whose voice still lingered in my head.

I was returning from a follow-up visit to an artist who had applied for funding at the foundation I worked for. The discussion about her project had been a joy: her practice had been consistent over the years, and she had a good story to tell. It was clever, as well as politically and socially relevant to the present context; all things the Covert Foundation would be glad to support. The visit had taken longer than expected. My background as an art critic in London interested her.

We had ended up talking about artists whose work she felt close to, and discussed exhibitions one of us had seen and the other had missed. We spoke about people we both knew and listed galleries or museum spaces she might be able to show her final project at. These kinds of encounters helped me to bridge my past and present lives. Years before, as a young, idealistic art critic, I would have derided the kind of art bureaucracy that my current job was all about, with its reports, application forms and select committees. But years down the line, after moving abroad and realising that neither art criticism, nor teaching, let alone freelance curating were exactly viable career options, I was grateful for a part-time job that allowed me to travel around the country occasionally and become acquainted with an art scene that I wanted to be included in.

Surprisingly, at some point in the conversation the artist had brought up the dating app. She said that one day it would be seen as a social experiment, and that she was considering using it for a new art piece. She liked the arbitrariness of the encounters she could make with it, and the randomness resonated with the rules that she based her multimedia installations on. She hoped it could lead to uncovering a hidden history of the city through the thousand stories those strangers would tell her.

Following her directions, I first downloaded Facebook to create an identity under an assumed name, so as to then connect it to the app and create a profile there. I liked the idea of an alter ego of sorts, to glide between identities, and keep a certain privacy. My new name would have to be international-sounding and work in different languages, but familiar, too, to Dutch speakers: Emma, maybe, a name that had recently topped the charts for baby names in the country, or Ada, after Nabokov's ardent heroine. Then I discovered I needed an age, an occupation and a few photographs: the very basics of an online identity. On an app where most users were said to be millennials, forty-five seemed out of place, unimaginable. I paused, typed thirty-nine. Looked at it, erased it. Typed forty-three. I would try and see, be truthful about my age, give or take a couple of years.

I looked up. The carriage, almost empty at first, was getting busier, picking up at each stop older men and women dragging shopping trolleys, presumably on their way to the open-air market on the Dapperstraat. I went back to the phone screen: the profile wanted its boxes to be ticked. 'Occupation': 'researcher' sounded vague . . . Vague enough or too vague? 'Art critic' might get me into fiery art discussions, and that was certainly not the point. It was a filtered randomness I was after. I wanted to give myself over to the algorithm, and discover the kind of people I had not yet come across in Amsterdam, people I would not meet in the art world. Maybe also men and women of my generation, not that of Anton and his friends, who were all over fifty.

I had to brand myself, so much I understood. 'Arts administrator' was far too dull, and it was only temporary, or so I hoped. 'Teacher' might awaken domination fantasies but that career option had been sampled and abandoned long ago. Eventually, I typed in 'Art historian, researcher': vague enough, but intriguing, with a bit of luck. 'Researcher' was accurate, at least, so far as the app was concerned. The rare photos I could find on my phone in which I was neither with Anton nor with Victor would have to do as well. They were few and far between, as if my son had provided, in the past nine years, the only impetus to take pictures of me, and the years before that, I could not take a picture without Anton being somewhere in the frame. I would not put any of that hobbies crap, but just a list of interests, kept vague, and high-brow: books, architecture, design.

The tram now crossed the Linnaeusstraat and glided along the far end of the Oosterpark, occasionally brushing against the bare lower branches of the park's monumental planes. On the other side of the street, South Indian and Surinamese food shops lined up along the sidewalk, in a continuous row occasionally punctured by a recently opened trendy bar. I searched for one that I knew, Bar Bukowski. It should be somewhere along this portion of the street, the one that had changed the most since I had discovered this part of town a few years back. The downpour continued and people step-ping onto the dry tram exhaled with visible relief, slogging down the aisle as their dripping clothes swished about. Others prepared to step out, gripping umbrellas as if they were life rafts.

On the app, however, it was perpetually summer. It showed me men, and occasionally women, all between forty and forty-five, as I had requested. Many were dressed in swimming trunks, hiking shorts, or casual T-shirts and jeans, and wore sunglasses. They drank from beer bottles or sat in restaurants, looking tanned and happy; occasionally, an arm connected to an intentionally blurred female face sitting beside them. An entire sequence showed balding men on boats holding very large fish. I realized I didn't know anyone who ever went on fishing vacations. The prevalence of sports and holidays in the sun was confirmed swipe after swipe while the rain battered the windows of the tram. I went back to the settings and added a short line to my list of interests in the profile description: 'Not particularly interested in sports or travelling'.

The tram jolted as it reached the raised banks of the Amstel, and we crossed the muddied, agitated waters of the river. The landscape became a blur specked with picturesque lamp posts. Looking out as far as I could, I saw only water, river and sky, a sea of textured greyish-beige, animated by streaks of rain and the swirls they created on the surface of the river. The tram stopped, the doors opened and closed. In came a couple, tourists I presumed. Out went a group of Italian-speaking goths. I continued to swipe. Casual wear seemed to be the norm, although a few men photographed at wedding parties wore suits with flowers on their lapels. Necks bulged from shirt collars, muscled chests stretching their fabric. In front of me, a young father in a dripping rain poncho preceded by a small shy-looking boy boarded the tram. More to my taste, I thought. A banker appeared on the screen: swipe (left); a restaurateur: swipe (right, with hesitation); an estate-agent: swipe left (resolutely).

Poncho daddy stepped out of the tram without so much

as glancing in my direction. I continued to swipe away. More wide necks and reddening faces, more balding heads and hardly any women: that was evidently not meant to be, at least today. Instead, a whole age group gradually appeared on the screen: middle-aged men whose physiques were shaped by drink and exercise. I thought again of the found-footage video piece in the museum, and of the individuals the artist had excavated from the film archive, of those bodies that were coerced into performing for the camera, of those who were discovering it for the first time, of those who seemed to ignore it. Ethnography had wanted to scrutinize those 'other' bodies, and colonialism, to subject them to the power of Empire. The camera was a key technology to do just that. The photographs on my phone showed a different type of image-making: self-promotion in carefully calibrated shots that exuded the sitters' pleasure to display themselves and exhibit their well-fed exuberance.

The tram shunted across town, the rhythm of my swiping echoing the repeated motion of its doors opening and closing. New faces appeared and disappeared, one stop after the next. Swipe left. Tram stopping: I looked up, drowsily expecting to see the same faces walking down the aisle as the ones that succeeded one another on the screen. Doors open. Doors close. A very pretty redhead boarded the tram, eyes fixed on his phone. Could he possibly be on the dating app too? Just in case, I lowered the age range to include people in their thirties like him, I surmised, and swiped through cards with renewed enthusiasm. The boy on the tram wasn't anywhere to be seen on the app yet. He walked off at the next stop. But other redheads appeared on the phone. In their thirties, slimmer, most often sporting a decent amount of hair, their faces not so red. This younger age group seemed more promising. As we passed the Amsterdam Business School, a group of young women in headscarves and jeans came onto the tram, speaking animatedly and clutching books and notepads. Two Italian couples then boarded the carriage, middle-aged, in corduroys and puffy jackets. They seem nothing less than shocked by the Dutch weather. Clinging to the metal poles, they stared at the tram map pasted on the wall, repeating the names of the stops with their melodious accent. Swipe right. A match. And again. The app invited me to start a discussion. Now? It could wait. The phone vibrated again, impatiently, to get my attention. For now, the swiping was intoxicating enough. All these happy smiling faces of available, attentive young men, who all seemed to be running mud races or riding race bikes, on holiday or sitting casually at a terrace in Amsterdam, seemed to be full of possibilities.

•

Those pictures came flowing back into my mind a few days later when Timo, a bald, chestnut-eyed software engineer in his late thirties delicately untied my belt, as he would a package that required careful unwrapping. Minutes before, I had been following him, heart pounding, as he cycled along the narrow streets behind the Kostverlorenkade canal. I had finally understood the implications of what I had innocently asked him back at the café. He was one of my first matches on the dating app and the conversation had been easy-going, teasing and clever. I knew the place he had proposed to meet at the next evening: café De Pels on the Huidenstraat. It was a drinking hole for old Amsterdam intellectuals by day. I was surprised to discover that it turned into a loud student hangout at night. The old-timers still held sway at the back, wax-like, under the glare of the salvaged lighthouse lamp hanging low over the rustic table filled with glasses of jenever and beer, slices of liver sausage and the newspapers of the day.

Over a couple of Laphroaig whiskies, Timo took pains to explain how the algorithm of the app worked, and when I observed how strange it was that our discussion was mainly revolving around it, he answered, without missing a beat:

'This is the thing: statistically people talk about what they have in common, so it's pretty normal for people who have never met except on the app to talk about it.'

I was still considering his unquestionable logic when I asked, without thinking, if we could go somewhere quieter. He paid for the drinks, and as we walked out, he suddenly gave me a peck on the lips before going to unlock his bike without a word. Startled, I went to unlock mine and we set off before I was able to ask what place he had in mind. Only when we reached a small metal bridge called the Buysbrug did I suddenly understand that 'go somewhere quieter', as I had proposed, was like a code phrase for 'I'd like to go back to your place'. Of course. Not that this hadn't been my aim all evening, but strangely, I'd been so absorbed in thinking about how to make it happen that I had not realized I had passed the threshold. And now, cycling away behind this broad-shouldered software engineer, it felt like I had gotten seriously ahead of myself.

I had obviously pulled it off in the café, saying little, and letting him take centre stage. I had been detached yet inter-ested, rather cool, I thought, and sexy enough, with those heels that killed me. But now I realized I had left some crucial bits of information out. He could not know that I was out of practice in 'that' department – extramarital sex, I began to think, anxiously – or that I still had pregnancy stretch marks all over my hips and belly and quite a few kilos to shed. I didn't have time to warn him about my breasts, either. They had been glorious in the past, but since the birth of Victor, they stubbornly pointed downwards. As Timo stopped and pointed to the circular-shaped block of flats in front of us, I smiled uneasily, pulled out my phone and asked him, with as cool a tone as I could manage, for the exact address so that I could text it to my husband.

'I always let him know where I am, so he'll know where to start looking if I don't come home.' I smiled weakly, tapping away the address he gave me.

'... And since you said you like architecture, do you know that this street, Van der Palmkade, is actually the only privately owned street in Amsterdam?' He explained the administrative glitch that had made this possible when the massive complex had been built just over a decade earlier at the intersection of three canals. 'It's called the Meander. Come, you will see it better from upstairs.'

He preceded me up the staircase: 'This used to be a candle

factory, this site I mean, part of an industrial estate dating as far back as to the seventeenth century. It was pulled down over time, as the city expanded. The only thing left is the old sawmill that we passed by on the other side of the water, just after the bridge. Did you notice it?' He interrupted his ascent and turned around.

I mumbled non-committally as I followed him up the spiral staircase. No, I had not seen the sawmill. At this precise moment, I felt so nervous that I had altogether no idea where I was. I was still mystified by the cool boldness I had displayed earlier, and suddenly confused as to how and what had brought me to this strange place with this strange person.

He droned on: 'The building is full of families, really, and there's even a crèche on the ground floor. I bought it when I was expecting to live here with my girlfriend, but that did not work out, so right now, I have a flatmate, also a software guy.'

He grinned, opening the door to a sparsely furnished apartment. 'It is a little weird, I think we are the only two bachelors in the whole complex.'

'You live with someone! Shouldn't we go say hello to him?'

He seemed a little taken aback.

'OK, sure, let's . . . see how he is doing.'

The unnamed flatmate was slumped on a swivel chair at his desk, his back to the door, surrounded by a forest of computer screens. He seemed to be simultaneously working and watching the daily reruns of the Sochi games, a beer in hand. He turned around, unsurprised to see a strange woman in his house, and greeted us.

'Hi there. Still working on the bank assignment. I'll probably be at it all night. So, see you later, Tim.'

Timo guided me to the other end of the flat, to a large
circular-shaped room with floor-to-ceiling windows that I
immediately walked up to. The sky was clear and the moon
glowered over the three canals that intersected at the foot of
the Meander.

'What are they called?' I asked, gesturing at the canals,
mouth dry, hands moist. I just needed him to continue speaking, about anything, really, to buy time while I calmed down.

'And, may I have a glass of water please?

I gulped the water down as he pointed at 'the Kattensloot,
directly opposite us. The Kostverlorenvaart we cycled by on
the way here. And the one to the left here is the Wittenkade.'
He spoke quietly, standing close behind me.

'The view is really wonderful,' I murmured, 'especially
with the full moon, it's so bright, there's no need to turn
lights on.'

I turned around, and without thinking, just to break the
tension, I pressed my lips onto his. They were warm, full, and
he kissed back confidently, sliding from my lips to my neck,
tenderly pushing away my hair. He caressed my hand and
placed it into his. We walked to his bed.

His touch, the touch of a stranger with whom I shared
nothing but this precise instant electrified me. I tried to
focus on the objects around the room to steady myself, to
attune to the moment and the place. In the semi-darkness I
identified a tall potted plant, several computers, a race bike
and a music keyboard lying on the floor. I turned my sight

from one to the other, and back again, repeating the successive glances, as if the objects formed a rebus the solution of which would magically help me adjust to the situation. Somewhere overlooking three canals, I stood in the arms of a flat-sharing software engineer (a software engineer, really?) who was unhurriedly relieving me of my jacket, my cardigan and everything else between kisses and caresses. But there was nothing to explain, nothing to justify: each of my actions had been entirely deliberate, even if they had momentarily anticipated my actual thinking, considering, deciding. I was there because I wanted to taste the skin of this random software guy.

I sat down and Timo held me by the waist as I leant back onto the cold sheets; stretching my arms across the bed, lying perfectly still, slowing down my breathing. Methodically, he moved his hands up and down my thighs in firm caresses, first through the fabric, and then on my bare skin. Suddenly he pushed his face in between my legs, inhaling me deeply.

I gasped and tried to hold on to the sight of the keyboard, the bike, the potted plant, tangible things around me, things I could understand as my body began to tingle. A sudden warmth between my legs turned into a dart in my lower belly that sent ripples across the rest of my body. Timo cupped my breasts, caressed them, kneaded them. I wondered briefly why the race bike was in his bedroom, and turned my eyes again to the potted plant. Its form, outlined by the cool moonlight, projected a giant spidery shape across the floor and on the walls. My breath became shorter, quicker and then I heard a moaning, increasingly loud and urgent, next to Timo's even breathing. And then suddenly everything in me seemed to give way, to quiver, spears shooting through in all directions. I wanted to push him away and grab him; kiss him, take his bald head into my arms, press it against my breasts, press him again down into me. I wanted him to be inside me and I wanted to push everything out at the same time. The intensity of the orgasms surprised me. It was as if they rippled and echoed the intensity of that first touch, the surprise, the fantasy it awakened of physical intimacy with a total stranger.

The streets were empty when I left his house a couple of hours later. He had insisted on getting dressed again and had walked me to my bike. On the way home I exulted, whizzing through the bright frosty night. I had found a lover! It would be perfect: I could easily go back to his place for a few orgasms once or twice a week. As I rode across the city, I plotted the best route from my home to his, from his to the foundation, from his to any part of town. It was easy to find, in that old industrial part of town, past the old sawmill. How could I have felt so disoriented a moment ago? I had been so nervous, and then it had been so powerful, that feeling of not knowing what would happen or how it would happen; the slight sense of danger, and then, the way the intensity gave way to complete release, total pleasure. He probably didn't work office hours; he would often be free, then. I wasn't sure how to take the next step, something to figure out tomorrow. I snuggled into bed next to an already sleeping Anton. I would tell him all about it in the morning.

●

'Friday night was so nice. Shall we try again sometime soon?'

I sent the message, casual and light, interested but not forceful, I thought, as I stood in the long queue at the Sunday farmer's market. Anton and Victor were having a father-and-son moment with cinnamon-sprinkled apple pie at the café around the corner. I felt the phone's discreet vibration in my coat pocket on the way home. A prompt answer, then. 'Yes, it was super nice' said the first line that glinted on the locked screen. Promising enough. The rest could wait. There were groceries to unpack, lunch to make, and Victor's afternoon playdate coming soon.

Hours later I stared at the unlocked screen.

'Yes, it was super nice! Thanks for meeting up. For me though it's a one-time only thing. Hope you don't mind. Take care.'

I read the message again, slowly taking in each word. That evening, when I opened the app again, I could no longer find Timo in the list of men I had been chatting with recently. Silly, they must be organized alphabetically. I scrolled again and again: was his name even listed as Timo? Maybe not. I tried to remember, but there was no need. Timo had disappeared; he had 'unmatched' me, as the proper name for this was.

Somewhere in a circular-shaped room in the complex known as the Meander, near the picturesque old sawmill that sits on the edge of the Kostverlorenvaart, the wide canal that used to mark the edge of the city, was a race bike, a potted plant whose shadow in the moonlight drew giant spider shapes on the floor, and a keyboard on the ground; I knew the shortest cycling route from my home to that room. But its occupant had vanished. There was another way to put it: I had been unceremoniously dumped by my first ever online sex date.

4

Platform Thinking

'Thank you for joining us, Gabrielle, I am not sure you know everyone around the table? Here is Akwasi from digital media, Marta from press and marketing development, Koen here is specialized in VR adapted to commercial use. Setiawati is our design historian and head of research, Jelmer our head of publications and Merel our exhibitions director,' they each nodded in turn, somewhat mechanically.

'. . . in short, a bunch of brilliant people . . . far more brilliant than myself, if I may say so.' David chuckled affably.

'Now allow me the pleasure of introducing you to everyone. Gabrielle and I met a couple of years ago at a conference in London. I had not yet joined the Design Museum. By coincidence, I had just read her wonderful book about contemporary art and archives – I mentioned this to most of you. We got speaking and then I realized that you lived, not in London or Paris as I had imagined . . . but right here in Amsterdam! Gabrielle currently works for the Covert Foundation which, as you know, gives out funding to artists' projects, in addition to her beautiful exhibition curating practice.' He paused for effect. His overly honeyed tone always made me feel ill at ease. 'Gabrielle has, in other words, a great expertise in the field of contemporary art, as well as experience with making exhibitions. And this is why,' he said, turning towards me, 'we thought you were exactly the right person to contribute to this new project. My hope is that you will add an intellectual gravitas at the same time as a fresh contemporary art outlook on the more technical, political and social issues that we want to address in the project.'

David slowed down the flow of his speech to better emphasize certain words – 'gravitas', 'fresh', 'technical', and so on – in a manner that endowed them with a sense of urgency. Spoken by others they would seem banal, but by him, they sounded groundbreaking. This particular, affected, way of speaking played no small part, I suspected, in his enduring success running museum institutions across the country.

There were polite smiles around the table. I was too accustomed to being the outsider in an institution not to recognize, behind the grinning faces, curiosity mixed with the worry that I would weigh them down, want to do things differently, and even that, favoured by the boss, I might win small but essential arbitrations further down the line, as the project took shape. Permanent museum staff never particularly enjoy the prospect of a freelance curator joining an existing team.

David was speaking again.

'You could say this project is an exhibition slash workshop slash lecture series slash expert meeting.' He looked around him, smiling, and the staff beamed, each one realising that their input would be on an equal footing with the other's. The marvels of people management.

'And what we are interested in exploring' – again, the emphasis on the key words – 'is very simply the impact of digital technology on our everyday lives. We have seen many projects about people and computers in the past, and we don't want to redo that kind of thing.' He briefly adopted a comically bored look:

'There has been a lot already about that: brilliant shows about the surveillance society blah blah bah, others about the history of the computer. But we are not doing Deep Blue plays chess against human again! Of course, there will be some historical component, perhaps that's for the conference, or the publication?' He looked at Jelmer and Marta who nodded approvingly.

'It is really this contemporary moment that we want to capture, to invite people to think about. After all, this is exactly what makes our difference, here, on this square, from the other museums that surround us.'

David turned around and looked through the large window overlooking the Museumplein. Directly across the expanse of grass stood the Stedelijk Museum, with its brand-new, smooth white extension, immediately nicknamed by the locals 'de badkuip', the bathtub. The Van Gogh Museum was on the right, with its semi-buried half-moon-shaped extension, surrounded by swarms of people queuing, and its staff herding the crowds in bright yellow raincoats and matching umbrellas. At the far end of the triangle, surrounded by formal gardens, the

Rijksmuseum signalled itself by its Renaissance-Gothic turrets. The Design Museum was the most recent addition to the Museumplein. It sat in a renovated mansion next to the American Consulate. David had lobbied for its creation and then for its present location on the museum square for years, and was keenly aware of the challenges he faced in such an exposed location.

'In a nutshell, the premise of the show, the backstory, if you will, that we want to share with our audiences is the story of how we have moved from the idea that computers are these very sophisticated tools that process data for us, and now basically enable people to run the world, to the idea that computers affect and change our way of being, our way of living, in short, our whole experience of the world.' David paused to let the words sink in, looking more guru-like, with his shiny bald head, than ever.

'There is a process going on right now, as we speak, in 2014, in this country, and our aim is to capture and make sense of it. Netflix, for instance, is fast-growing. Until last year, it was only available in the United States, but in September it launched in the Netherlands, the first country outside the USA.' As he spoke, I suddenly remembered a phrase that was everywhere on profiles throughout the dating app: 'Netflix and chill'. So that is what it was about.

'There are technical as well as cultural reasons that make the Netherlands a hotspot for the development of digital media from the United States. Akwasi here is the specialist, and perhaps you could tell us a few words about this?'

I knew Akwasi, a Ghanaian-British digital media

specialist, a little already, via David who had recruited him via his extensive London network.

'OK, so, I will try to draw a picture of ongoing developments and of the importance of the Netherlands on the world map of internet connections, and not get too technical about it.' Akwasi paused, rolled up one of his shirtsleeves and delved into a technical explanation of the Amsterdam Internet Exchange. He explicated patiently how underseas cables had criss-crossed the oceans since the beginnings of the telegraph and how the most recent internet cables followed more or less those routes.

'There are a few points, a few nodes in Europe where the cables from the United States and other distant places come together: Stockholm, München and ... yup, Amsterdam. It's one of the biggest hubs for internet traffic worldwide. The Amsterdam Internet Exchange, or AIE, is located in Science Park, near the Amsterdam–Rhine Canal, and was for a long time only part of an academic network, that is, until after 1992, with the privatization of the internet, under the Clinton-Gore administration. Dot com money began to flow in, and American internet giants have been steadily moving into the Dutch market with new media and digital platforms since then. The Netherlands became the favourite testing ground for American new media companies.'

He smiled, congenially. 'We are a small country, highly connected to the internet, with a large proportion of the population that speaks English and there is this hardware connection, the AIE. Next to Netflix, Amazon is about to launch an online book and magazine rental service that works with their Kindle. Companies like these have betted successfully on the idea that people are happy to switch from owning to renting cultural content. And the same, of course, is happening with music, with platforms like Napster and Spotify. The latter has taken off over here in the past few months. And then there are new things, like the flat rental platform, Airbnb, which monetizes the concept of "couch-surfing". They received official authorization to start operating in Amsterdam just a few weeks ago. It's bound to change the way people think about home ownership and travelling. The list goes on, with platforms that are gradually changing the way we live, think and consume. The dating market is another example: Grindr is pretty niche, but Tinder aims to reach a wider market. It is becoming really mainstream. And ergonomically, these dating apps are interesting: you "swipe" profiles, like this.' He mimed the gesture, swiping his right-hand index finger across the palm of his left hand.

'Thanks, Akwasi!' David boomed. 'All these new platforms make up the backbone of what is usually called the "sharing economy", or "platform economy", and Amsterdam is the perfect place to reflect on what is happening, how it is happening, and what it's doing to our lives. This peering point, the AIE, means that the city is a strategic location in Europe for the development of the digital economy. We are going to address this in a number of ways, and I think Setia is the best person to explain it further. Would you mind?'

'Sure,' Setiawati looked around as she stood up and fished her iPhone from her pocket. She cradled it in her interlaced fingers like a piece of evidence. 'Since the advent of smart-phones, and even more, since 2003, when the first iPhone with a front-facing camera was launched, the platform economy has grown exponentially. The selfie-camera boosted media, such as Facebook, Instagram, Twitter and so on, by making it possible for people, through selfies, to embed themselves into social media. This has accelerated what media historian and anthropologist Sherry Turkle had earlier described as the transformation of "a machine on the border of becoming a mind". What interests us is how this machine that becomes a mind affects the mind of the human who operates it. How do people's behaviours change through and with these objects and media, and what does this concept of the sharing economy mean, in historical, social, political and philosophical terms?'

She paused and looked around to see if there were any comments, and continued.

'We are primarily a design museum, so our starting point will be a history of the object, of the design that makes the object desirable, and then indispensable. We are interested in "intimate" histories of objects – again a topic that Sherry Turkle wrote about before many others. And from there on we move to studying more immaterial issues; ideological, sociological and so on. Koen will organize workshops next to the exhibition, as well as an expert meeting on media regula-tion. In short, each section of the show will address a different aspect. We will have a presentation on biometrics, one about GPS technology and applications, about music videos, and contemporary art: this is where you come into the project, Gabrielle?' she concluded.

'Exactly,' David answered with a wide grin, turning towards me. 'Your work on the subject of the archive as a concept and a technology of preservation, and your knowledge of the current art scene, is the reason we have asked you to join us. We would love you to curate a section of the show presenting artists who respond to these issues of the digital and everyday life.'

●

After the meeting ended, Merel and Jelmer walked me through the building while we discussed the practicalities of contracts, planning, and deadlines. I had a few months to come up with a plan, till after the summer holidays, and was glad to be invited to organize an exhibition. This was more challenging than anything the Covert Foundation had ever asked me to do.

My studio visits for the Foundation were something akin to fine-tuning. I would keep silent at first. I listened to artists and looked around. I would try to figure out what had been going on between the four walls of the studio, and then give pointers about applying for funding. Sometimes it was like finding the missing bolt or screw to make the whole project work. I would suggest a book to read, mention a news item or make a simple remark about everyday life. Or I would ask about a specific work, attempt to find gaps in their narrative and help them strengthen their project and their application.

Exhibition curating, on the other hand, was like creating a world for others to experience, a world furnished with ideas, images and objects collected along a thinking process and which together told a story. Of course, there would be limitations and it irked me that contemporary art was so often pigeonholed and made to fit a purpose, given a particular task to perform. Perhaps Saskia, the artist who wanted to work with the dating app, should be my first stop to discuss possibilities. David and Setia's brief suggested my response needed to be more than a neat selection of half-a-dozen up-and-coming artists surfing a wave of art and tech. A decade or so ago, even more perhaps, robotics had been a trend in the art world. It was practised almost exclusively by young white nerdy male artists: 'boys with toys' as I called them in my articles for art magazines.

My recent experience with the dating app on the tram had nothing to do with robotics – it was a more troubling experience. For a few instants, the pictures that I swiped away one by one on the screen of my phone had superimposed themselves seamlessly onto the real world, replacing or adding to what I saw directly in front of me. Even their motion of appearing and disappearing on the screen uncannily mimicked the way passers-by on the tram, and later on the street, appeared in my visual field and then disappeared from it, as if swiped away by an imaginary finger.

These new technologies were more intimate than the earlier desktop computers modelled after analogue bureaucratic paraphernalia such as the office desk, the blackboard and the filing cabinet. The new devices and their software operated more fluidly through a motion of easy give and take between the virtual and the real. They accompanied and enhanced the movements of our eyes, replaced the maps, the watches and the books we used to carry around with us. Increasingly they came to answer each of our needs and questions, to fill narrow interstices in our life that we did not even know existed with things we did not know we needed.

I thought again about Fiona Tan's montage film, which I had seen at the museum a few days before, with its haunting colonial and ethnographic footage. It really was about the way people adapt to a new technology at the same time as they endure colonial power. The opening sequence, that I had just caught when I entered the gallery, with its motionless groups of military men aligned as if they were posing for a photograph, when in fact they had been filmed by a camera, showed one of these moments where a posture that has become habitual to one technology is suddenly transferred to another, newer one. That static posing of the men in turbans and the colonial officers showed a moment of discrepancy, a moment of shift from one technology to the other, and how bodies respond to that shift. Gradually and imperceptibly, they would adapt to the changes and then learn to manipulate these new technologies, so that they eventually turned into mere extensions of a natural gesture.

Setiawati had efficiently summarized the history of portable computing in her short presentation, mentioning objects so outdated now that 'nobody remembers them today'. Some of them had been struck prematurely by technological obsolescence, before they had a chance to take off commercially. Others had been plagued from the start by ergonomic mismatch.

'Who remembers today,' she had said with a smile

directed, I felt, at the oldest of us in the room, 'the PalmPilot and the Psion?' Their evocation had triggered blurred memories of difficult connections and clumsiness. Still, I had loved my little Psion, a tiny word processor that I had used two decades earlier as a fledgling art critic, when I travelled around Europe to see exhibitions and typed up my articles sitting on trains.

I left the Design Museum mulling over these thoughts and walked across the sprawling lawn of the Museumplein. I stopped in the middle of the frosted turf. Here the sounds of the city became suddenly muted and you could feel at a remove from the surrounding agitation. Street lamps were coming on, and trams and buses crowded the corner occupied by the neoclassical façade of the Concertgebouw. Away from the noise of the street, I suddenly thought again of a recent occasion, at the Stadsschouwburg, the city theatre, where a stifled silence had been infused with a comparable sense of expectation. It was during those few minutes that followed the moment when the audience, having finally settled into their seats, became silent and attentive to the signs that the performance was about to begin. It was then that Anne Teresa De Keersmaeker had walked casually onto the stage and put the vinyl record on, before she started to dance in front of the record player. I understood now why I had been transfixed by the scene. That gesture of lowering the arm of the record player, and then the scraping sound of the needle, came from a faraway time and space.

It was a pre-digital gesture, a gesture from which an analogous sound emerged. Both the sound and the movement that triggered it were as antiquated as the clicking of a camera, the winding sound of a rotary phone dial and the mechanical noise of a hand-wound camera being cranked up. At the beginning of the performance Keersmaeker had reactivated the remembrance of one of those archaic objects whose uses are buried somewhere in our memories. In triggering it, she had metaphorically summoned countless other outmoded things like telephones and cassette players that were both intimate and deeply social, and that eventually became obsolete as technology moved on.

When they disappear, those antiquated objects leave us with memories of gestures which are like phantom pains that eventually go away when we learn how to operate newer devices. Replaying the dance sequence in my head, I realized that it revealed something that fascinated me when I thought about life in the digital age and its rapid succession of inventions. A simple and banal gesture like playing a record could suddenly activate a lost memory, conjure it from the depths of the past, and convey a sense of time gone by. For a moment, then, the vibrancy of lived experience, its overwhelming quality could cut through the flatness of life through a smartphone. The summoning of past gestures made us realize the unnaturalness of new ones: tapping on a phone, swiping, speaking with earphones; gestures that had seemed at first forced, as they propelled our reluctant selves into the future.

'Who today remembers the PalmPilot and the Psion?' Setiawati, all youth and brains, had raised one of the paradoxes of the digital age. That in it we become amnesic while at the same time the machines that surround us record every move we make. Infinite memory and infinite amnesia: two sides of the same coin.

I began to walk across the expanse of green again, the frosted blades of grass creaking under each step. As I came near the beginning of the Paulus Potterstraat, at the corner of the Hobbemastraat, I was back in the hum of the city, amidst hurried passers-by navigating bicycles and cars.

•

'Arrived early at café, but please don't rush, all relaxed here! Looking forward to meeting you. PS look for the guy with very light blond hair and sleepy eyes!'

It was lunchtime the following Thursday and I was on my fourth new date in as many days. I spotted Heiko immediately, sat in the middle of the Portuguese café. Slouched over a mug of steaming coffee and a pastel de nata, he was rubbing his eyes when I introduced myself and joined him at the table. For a few instants, I just sat there, straight as a stick, looking at him. I was still on a high from the hectic morning routine at home and waiting for Anton's daily message confirming Victor had arrived safe at school. I glanced at my phone again, but nothing.

Heiko, wispy and charming, asked if everything was OK. Victor had gotten better at cycling and was now eager to ride to school on his own, but I insisted that Anton still bike with him before he continued on to his office. A few months before, a little girl had been hit by a rubbish truck cycling to school. I was terrified. And Victor refused to wear a helmet. Everyone wears them in London, I'd insisted. 'Nobody does in Amsterdam, you would look like a proper dork,' father and son had replied in chorus. I tried to push those thoughts away. It was probably all fine, Anton would never let Victor go on his own without telling me.

I focused on the young man sitting across from me at the table. He was somewhere in his early thirties, short, with washed-out blue eyes, an unconvincing thin moustache and longish hair so fair it was almost white. His chunky slate-grey turtleneck framed a pointy face and emphasized the paleness of his eyes. He had warned me beforehand: he managed a cocktail bar and so meeting up would need to happen either around two or three in the morning after the bar closed, or in that short timespan between his getting up around lunchtime and going to work: in our chat on the app, we had joked about the different time zones we seemed to live in, in one same city. Anton's text finally brightened my screen. Victor was in school. All was well.

Behind the bar, the staff busied themselves. Smoky-salty scents of bacalhau and potato croquette, brought in from the kitchen on large tin trays, filled the air; the swing doors banged; the coffee machines hissed and gurgled, interrupted by the screeching of the coffee grinder. The sun hit the blue and white wall tiles with a pallid hue through the small windowpanes of the café, a cosy enclave in the middle of the red-light district, on the Geldersekade canal.

Heiko was speaking animatedly about his cocktail bar, the crowdfunding campaign that had helped with the original financing, the years of training in bars across town, his fascination and dedication to nightlife in the big city – big at least for the young Frisian who had grown up in a tiny village populated mostly by sheep. He asked questions about my life in Amsterdam – the smallest city I had ever lived in, I teased in return, citing Paris and London, where I had grown up and studied. He radiated a curious mix of boyishness and maturity, the latter, I surmised, owing to the sense of duty that comes with business ownership. That contrast became increasingly visible as the conversation went on, and gradually I became aware that under the surface of a casual flirting game with jokes and a few compliments thrown in for good measure, there was a more straightforward exchange between two adults who knew exactly the reason of their meeting up.

There was a frankness I had not often encountered in the past week or so when I had, thanks to the dating app, met up with half a dozen men for afternoon coffees and short evening drinks. The most recent one, I had not even attempted to engage in conversation with. Arriving a little late, as I always did, I had spent a few minutes observing him through the window of the café. Men on dates tended – I was learning this fast – to sit in conspicuous spots, in clear view of the door, and check their phone repeatedly for pictures of the person they were expecting. The one who waited for me that evening looked so bulky and mannish that I had not had the nerve to walk in and meet him. There was no chance this would work. So I had retreated into the shadows outside of the bar and texted an apology. A migraine had declared itself on the way and I was now back home. I would not make it, I was very sorry, I would be in touch. I waited twenty-four hours and then made him disappear in a click.

Sitting opposite Heiko, I would have never said he was my type. But then I didn't think I had one – at least not knowingly, contrary to some of my friends who baffled me by their parochialism when they described their type down to hair or skin colour and sporting activities. But next to his elusive waifish allure, Heiko displayed a self-assuredness and honesty that I immediately liked. He was a good decade younger than me, according to his profile, but the age question never came up. There was nothing coy under his playfulness, so that when he came to ask me, point-blank, what I was after, since I was married albeit in an open marriage, I had not been afraid to reply just as directly:

'Sex.'

He smiled and slowly took a sip of his coffee.

'I am happy with that. I live upstairs, above the café. Do you want to come up now?'

His apartment was right at the top of the seventeenth-century merchant house, an attic flat full of wooden beams and a roof terrace to be accessed via a ladder. There was no need for small talk, although I felt a mix of apprehension and desire as he took my hand to guide me to his bedroom. I lay down, head propped up by a pillow, and he stretched like a cat across the width of bed, lying at my feet, holding up his face with his cupped hand. Looking straight into his serious gaze, without a word exchanged, I removed my underwear, lifted my skirt a little and touched him with the tips of my bare toes. He did nothing at first, just lay there, his whitish blond head resting on his elbow. Slowly he caressed my legs and delicately pushed them open. He looked intently at my cunt, as I looked at him. He began to stroke it carefully, as if attempting to reassure a skittish animal. I felt a moisture immediately as his fingers delicately opened the labia and slid inside of me, slightly rubbing the swelling flesh. I looked at him, concentrated, focused. Like a potter at his wheel, I thought, with no idea where that comparison came from. He was gathering pace but keeping his gestures measured, under control as I felt a growing dull tingle. I sensed him carefully attuning himself to the reactions of my body, noticing each small tremor that came across it. All the nervousness that I had felt earlier at the café and on my way up the stairs was now feeding my sexual arousal. He observed my vagina contracting, opening and closing – 'like a sea anemone', he later described it. He pressed a finger lightly over the labia and rubbed inside the vagina in a precisely gauged gesture.

I closed my eyes. The image of the potter at his wheel returned, and I could see a vessel taking shape, smooth and slippery between his hands, slowly growing taller and fuller as water began to swish and gush from the stirring wheel. I opened my eyes. A warm fluid trickled onto my thighs as Heiko rubbed a precise point inside the vulva, smiling at what he was provoking, staring with his large opalescent eyes.

'I think we need a towel here,' he said, mischievously. Without letting me out of eyesight he carefully placed a faded Spiderman beach towel under me and over the bed sheets.

'Do you always squirt as much as this?'

'I don't know.' It felt awkward to suddenly resume speaking. 'I think it's happened a few times,' I murmured, hesitantly, 'but I don't know, I am not sure ... I thought it was difficult to do, that only some women could do that, squirt.'

'Every woman can. It's a technical thing. It's just that most guys are a bit hopeless. It's mechanical, see. I bet you that within ten seconds you can squirt again, just as much.'

It was such an immature thing to say, and I wanted to answer that I was not a squeaky doll for him to play with, but immediately, as he rubbed again in the same place, I was stunned to feel a hot liquid surging from within. And again. The ejaculation became stronger each time, gushing out of my body.

'Hmm, we might need a bucket,' he teased. Each time, this new sensation created a warm, tranquil pleasure. Not an orgasm, at first. Rather, an unknown feeling of release, of letting go, of abandoning myself to a warm protective environment. Heiko seemed fascinated by what had turned into something sea-like, swollen and relaxed. He rubbed with the palm of his hand, slipping, spreading the wetness all over, and slid several more fingers inside me.

'Have you ever felt a whole hand inside of you?' he asked softly, showing me his hand, the tip of his fingers joined together, 'like this, would you like to try?'

'Yes ... I think so.' Whatever he was doing I wanted him to continue.

I tightened and then released my vagina around his fingers, keeping him inside, letting him come into me as his joined fingers and thumb began sliding through the wetness. I swayed, then lifted my hips to accompany the movements of his hand. There was a moment where my body seemed to close. Was it the pelvic bones marking a threshold? I panicked a little, and tried to visualize my anatomy, summoning a schoolbook diagram in shades of pink and white, and then the image of Victor's birth; of pushing him through and out. The memory of pressing my body to open for the head to appear, after which the rest of him had slipped out in a few seconds, came hurtling back from years earlier.

The cervix pushed the vagina to open, as Heiko's hand – his hand; that was such a very strange thought – glided inside me, his fist gently rocking inside. I had never felt anything as intense as this. Powerful orgasms rippled in succession, making my body quiver. A feeling of content-edness unfolded, along with a sentiment of fear that I could eventually overcome. Time ceased to exist. I was fully inside my body, sensing every motion of the closed hand inside. His movements triggered, strangely, excitement and calm at the same time. I stretched out my hand to feel his wrist between my legs. Slowly, with infinite precaution, he pulled his hand away. I felt his knuckles passing over the threshold, and sliding out. Like my newborn had once done, I thought again. Eyes closed, I dozed off. The sea anemone had fallen asleep. Time seemed to stretch infinitely.

A rustling sound of water woke me. A short while after-wards, I recognized the rumble of a coffee machine. More clatter of objects being moved, and then a strange, regular hissing sound, partly covered by free jazz music. I drowsily stepped out of the bed, dressed and walked into the living room to find Heiko half-clothed in colourful socks, a faded printed T-shirt and boxer shorts. He was ironing a shirt, his movements rhymed by the hissing of a steam iron that he deftly glided up and down the board.

He looked at me, concerned, and then down at his shirt. 'For the bar tonight. I should get going soon. And you need to drink water. You must be very dehydrated.' He smiled, pointing at a full glass on the table. 'I can also make you tea, if you like?' I slowly padded about the room, looked out of the window at the forest of jagged rooftops, turrets and church spires towards the Oude Schans, the old defensive moat of sixteenth-century Amsterdam. I slowly sipped my water.

'Thank you.' There was a rasp in my voice. I had been so intensely focused on the inside of my body that I had not realized how much I must have groaned and shouted.

'It was astonishing, what you can do, how I felt. It was really an experience. And we didn't even have . . .' I searched for the right word . . . '"conventional" sex. I got to do all the ejaculating,' I added, with a shy smile.

'That's OK, it was incredible to see your body move, the changing expressions on your face. It was beautiful, very sexy. The way you opened up, the way you relaxed and I could feel your pleasure. There is plenty of time to try "conventional sex" another day, if you would like that.'

Eyes fixed on the ironing board, I asked him how he did it, how he triggered those sensations.

'It's pretty simple.' Heiko carefully placed the iron on its side, before lifting his right hand in the air, the two middle fingers folded. 'See, this is how you need to hold your hand, and you need to rub, just inside, where you feel this more cushioned, spongy area. It's just a technique. Sometimes I see these good-looking guys on dates in my bar, guys who are so full of themselves that I am sure that they have never bothered to learn how to pleasure a woman.'

A bright ray of sun, shining low in the winter sky, caught me off guard as I reached the street. The days were getting a little longer, but I had no desire to stay out. I wanted to hold on to the overwhelming physical sensations I had experienced in the attic flat, in the hands of Heiko. Back home, I went straight up to our bedroom, curled up into a ball under the bedcovers and closed my eyes. During what felt like hours, I drifted in and out of half-sleep. I wanted time to stop, to let me remember with the greatest clarity and precision each and every second of the hours with Heiko. To remember, or more accurately to re-experience them.

I needed to be silent and motionless enough to perceive the faint echoes of the afternoon as they softly rippled through my body: the touch of Heiko's fingers on my bare skin, the intense wetness and the sensation of abandon. That visceral memory of giving birth that had surged out of nowhere. The slightly disturbing, but intensely satisfying experience of fisting, the absolute jubilation of ejaculating again and again: words that were new to me.

I wanted to sense again the intense release I had experienced in that bedroom, akin to swimming in the sea, and feel Heiko's unobtrusive presence, his hands and his voice awakening my body.

When I awoke, the sun had completely disappeared, the cold February night was seeping into the empty flat. Muffled sounds rose from the street: roaring, screeching, hooting: the twice-daily transportation of children and adults pouring out of schools and offices had begun: Anton and Victor would soon be back. I showered, dressed, turned the lights on and the heating up. It was time to return to everyday life and make dinner, when all the while I only wanted to go back to that sweet, soft liquid place that I had visited earlier that day.

5

Firewall Codes

The afternoon with Heiko on the Geldersekade had unlocked something. In the days that followed, when I still felt some stiffness in muscles I had not known existed, I sat at my desk to write an artist report and an exhibition review. But instead of working I found myself repeatedly drifting off and conjuring those few hours. Looking out at the rooftops outside the window of my study, I saw a different urban landscape from the view out of Heiko's top-floor apartment, but was carried back to his view as I tried to unpick the sensations of that afternoon, to understand what it had been about.

I remembered my hips swaying, the cervix pushing, my body opening up, the memory of giving birth suddenly fusing with a moment of sexual pleasure, as if sex could rewrite history, turn the pain of childbirth, the discomfort and absolute strangeness of putting another being into the world into something like a liberating gift. I remembered the drowsiness that followed the assaults of the repeated orgasms shaking my body. Yet there had been nothing like a shared

moment of climax with Heiko, in the sequence of gestures
and caresses. A sense of shared intimacy? I wasn't even really
sure. Although the pleasure had been perhaps greater in its
intensity to anything else I had ever experienced, that was not
exactly what had triggered the new awareness I could sense.
It had instead to do with giving myself over to him: letting
him observe, touch me, and trigger those sensations. I had
opened myself to being exposed, to losing control. That feeling had generated not uneasiness but, instead, it had brought
about a surprising sense of calm, a sense of letting go. I felt
as if I had gotten in a taxi in a foreign city like they did in
movies, and asked the driver to 'just drive.' Abandoning
volition and reacting only through sensations had generated
a profound sense of tranquillity, of joy.

And there was more. This process of letting go, of momentarily giving up willpower in the arms of a stranger made
me feel powerful rather than weak, in command, rather
than dominated. Giving myself over without holding back
was akin to saying 'I entrust you with my integrity'. It was
a gift of trust that resulted in his returning a gift, in a basic
anthropological sense. We had encountered each other
through that exchange, and to display myself in all naked
vulnerability had, surprisingly perhaps, given me potency, a
kind of self-confidence that I had never experienced before
that afternoon.

I tried to explain this to Anton, as we strolled amidst
the paintings of Marlene Dumas in an exhibition of her
work that had just opened at the Stedelijk Museum, but
the right words eluded me. Amidst Dumas's portraits of

fierce-looking women and her foreboding nudes I felt an even greater disconnect between this new experience of letting go and the posture of control that I assumed at work and in everyday life. I did not have the words to convey the intense sensations of that afternoon to Anton, who seemed anyway to want to concentrate on the paintings, admiring the intensity that emanated from the soft watery paint. In the end, instead of opening up about this new perception to my husband, I had made a feeble joke or two about Heiko's dexterity betraying his skill as a bartender. Anton had not asked for more information. If he had, I would have tried a little harder. He usually asked for a name, scraps of information, maybe an age, a location, the profession of the person I was seeing. I sometimes asked for more details. There were moments when I was curious about the kind of woman who appealed to him and who he desired. I googled them to find pictures and wanted to know how similar or different they were from me. There were other moments, though, where the only thing I wanted to know was what time he expected to be back home.

I met Heiko again a week later, and those few hours felt like a direct continuation of our first session. Again, it seemed that the extent of the pleasure I could feel had no boundaries. Again, I was mesmerized by his expertise, the uncomplicatedness of our interaction and the precision of his lovemaking. Again, his almost-total absence of emotion was odd but liberating: it was sex as precise exploration, and pleasure was an end in itself, not a gateway to intimacy, to shared experience, to togetherness. 'Session' was really the appropriate word to describe our moments together. Once more, I left his home feeling exhilarated and powerful and wanting to hold on to those precious moments.

But a short time after a third, similarly perfect meeting, there came a period where our calendars refused to sync. He would send messages in the dead of the night, when he finished work and closed the bar. He was thinking of me, picturing me moist and open. Would I like to come by, right now? I was of course deep asleep, alarm set to early in the morning. Or he texted at lunchtime when he woke up, from the warmth of his bed, suggesting that I should join him, saying that today he had a bit of time before his shift. Of course, I was always then in an endless studio visit, stuck at the other end of town, and it was raining. I sent messages in the evening when he was in the middle of his work shift and he wouldn't answer till hours later. I made a point of checking my phone around lunchtime and tried to leave my schedule open, but he was, increasingly, unavailable.

And so, I took the habit of dropping by the Portuguese café whenever I was in that part of town. I went there between studio visits and other appointments, at lunchtime or in the early afternoon. I stopped by for a cup of tea, a bacalhau croquette, a crispy Tentúgal, and the off-chance that his pale mop of hair would grace the white and blue chairs of the Portuguese café. I never deliberately set out to go there, but seemed to drift there involuntarily from other parts of town. I would park my bike under his windows and push open the door of the only place that held a connection, however tenuous, to him.

Once, on a busy Friday lunchtime, I was queuing at the bar, on high alert for all things Heiko, but ready to say I had dropped in on a whim. I went to grab my phone to text him an impromptu message when I heard my name called out.

'Gabrielle!'

The brief excitement disappeared as soon as I realized the voice was nothing like Heiko's. I looked around. Akwasi from the Design Museum was waving cheerfully from the other side of the room.

He had cosily set up camp at a corner table with a book and a large coffee. He gave me an amused smile as I approached, tilting the book cover for me to read it: Roland Barthes. *Camera Lucida. Reflections on Photography.*

'You found me out! I'm catching up on French theory!'

'Hi! So, indeed I see, is that for the "Digital and Everyday Life" project?'

'Yep. I am tired of Setiawati being the only intellectual at the museum! And everyone, including you, seemed to mention this book, so I thought I should give it a try.'

'You are right, it's beautiful. Do you like it?'

'It's pretty far from where I come from, and it's so damn melancholic in places, but the punctum, the punctum, man, it's a good one, this idea that a thing in a photo just grabs you, viscerally, just you personally.'

Akwasi clenched his fist as if grabbing the punctum as he spoke.

'Yes, I think about it as this idea that photographs hide, inside of them, small things in plain sight, personal messages addressed to each one of us. I love Barthes, it's just that I get a bit annoyed at the way that academics have taken hold of that word, "punctum", and then blown it up into a lifeless, generic concept. It kills it from the inside.'

'Oh yeah? Explain it to me.'

I stared down at the mosaic floor. Lecturing about Roland Barthes was the last thing I wanted to do right now, unless it magically gave Heiko a few extra minutes to appear, by chance, in the café.

'I mean: people here, in the UK, and especially in the US, call him a theorist, a philosopher, but really he was a critic, an essayist, first and foremost. The best thing about him is really the way he simply looks at things and shares personal impressions of them with the reader, the way he makes us witness and share his thinking process. That's the beauty of his best writing, at least for me. It's not the Roland Barthes who pontificates about signs that I like, it's the Barthes who smoked cigarettes and described how he tried to pick up younger handsome men at the Café de Flore.'

Akwasi looked a little taken aback. 'Understood. Well, you are a bit French after all!' He paused, looked around the café. 'Usual digs?'

'Nope. I was just passing through between meetings, and thought I would get a few pastries to take home.'

'Ah OK, you should, they are delicious, I'm often here.' He looked out at the street. 'I live just around the corner. The queue's getting shorter, you might want to jump right in.'

'Thank you.' I took a few steps towards the counter and turned around. 'By the way, how is the project going at the museum?'

'Ah, early days, early days. To be honest, I don't think even they know what they are doing yet,' he gave a cheeky smile, 'but you know, I'll come in a bit later on in the process, so maybe they are just leaving me in the dark for now. How's your part of the gig shaping up?'

'It's getting there,' I answered vaguely. 'I should get going. Nice to bump into you, let's have coffee when I am next over at the museum.' I muttered a few more platitudes and walked over to the counter, bought a couple of pastéis de nata and walked straight out, still clutching the phone in my coat pocket, feeling as if my longing for Heiko had been exposed.

•

The possibility of running into Akwasi at the Portuguese café again brought an end to my hanging around there, waiting for Heiko. I needed to busy myself with someone else until I could see him again, so I began to spend increasing amounts of time on the dating app. Sometimes I conscientiously clicked through each photograph of every profile that came up on the screen. I scrutinized faces, bodies and attitudes. I read the little texts when they were provided and then, holding my breath, I swiped right or left.

Most often, though, I swiped fast and carelessly, looking for what I had lost. Hidden within each face and each profile, I hoped, confusedly, to find Heiko again; to swipe right on him, to match, chat, and start it all over again.

Soon, however, the very gesture of swiping through dozens of profiles became satisfying in and of itself. It gave me a similar contentment to the one I felt when I got things done: when I crossed things out on a task list, cleared my desk or emptied the in-tray at work: the satisfaction of 'going through' stuff. I was aware that the fulfilment was never complete, that it always left a vague sense of lacking that made me return continuously to the dating app to swipe some more. As long as there were profiles on the app that I had not checked and crossed out, I had to go on, in search of that elusive and wholly ingrained feeling of bureaucratic achievement.

When I swiped briskly, I scanned the first picture of each profile for a few seconds, enough time for a detail in the image to move me, grab me, arouse or disgust me. I looked for a trigger that might be obvious and immediate, but that most often hid in the details and jumped out unpredictably. I focused my attention on the way that a detail in a picture called something up deep inside. I thought back to the conversation with Akwasi at the Portuguese café, of his fresh enthusiasm for Roland Barthes and that magical word, the punctum: that seemingly inconsequential detail that touches us when we look at a photograph. I was sure that if Barthes was around nowadays, he would be, just like me, going through photos of young men on some dating app or another, at a high enough speed to put his whole punctum idea to the test.

Barthes must have come up with the term intuitively, as he looked through a bunch of photographs scattered on his desk, before starting to write about photography, to write what would be his last book, *Camera Lucida*. I pictured him sitting at a white round Saarinen table he was once photo-graphed working at, sifting through the pictures. He would have paid attention to each image but also remained closely attuned to his own reactions, and noted the small feature within each image that pricked him and wounded him, as he described it, referring to the meaning of 'punctum' in Latin.

I tried to do the same. Within the space of a few seconds, I attempted to identify that pricking detail, and then decided what it meant to me. How fast could I decide to swipe right or to swipe left, yes or no, this one or that one, both, or nei-ther? In one picture, it was the eyebrows almost touching one another that moved me; in the next the way a T-shirt draped itself across a pair of shoulders. In a third, a graceful slouch. These small details, these manifestations of the punctum decided which way I would swipe.

'J'aime, je n'aime pas', I hummed in my head, swiping any-where and all the time. 'J'aime, je n'aime pas', I swiped, even as I stirred a risotto, or waited for the pasta to cook. 'J'aime, je n'aime pas': the title, I now remembered, of another exercise that Roland Barthes shared with readers, when he consigned a list of his likes and dislikes in this weird little autobiograph-ical book Anton had once given me, *Roland Barthes par Roland Barthes, Roland Barthes by himself.* I remembered Barthes liked marzipan and cinnamon, and disliked 'women wearing trou-sers', a point that showed him to be more conservative than I had expected. But never mind the banality of individual choices, he wrote. The whole point of the exercise was that these sums of likes and dislikes told us that we are each our own, that 'my body is not the same as yours', that no matter

how close we might be to someone, we always remained a
'bodily enigma' to the other.

The Roland Barthes swiping technique resulted in dozens
of matches, that each announced their arrival on the phone
with a cheerful little vibration. I went through them with
dedication over days and weeks – another bureaucratic
satisfaction – and I kept at least half a dozen conversations
going at the same time, some for hours, others for a few
days at most. I texted between things, waiting for a running
partner in the park, taking a break from work, as I ran a bath
for Victor.

I fed these exchanges with random thoughts, off-the-cuff
remarks that my interlocutors picked up or not. These conver-
sational ping-pongs faded or stopped when one of us made
a move to propose to meet. Timing was often of the essence:
there was always a moment, a blank in the exchange, where
things could go either way. To meet or not to meet. Some got
the tempo right while others did not. And then there was
the issue of attitude, of vocabulary. I expected them to be
original, smart, funny if they could and somehow sexy in
their messaging, but I instantly unmatched after any sexually
explicit question or remark.

Texting had a sensuousness of its own, I discovered. It
provided me with interlocutors by the dozen, random people
whom I imagined were close-minded, and with whom I
shared the permanent conversations I had in my head. Once
or twice perhaps, I think I said something aloud instead of
texting it, and Anton, who was reading on the sofa, lifted
his head up and looked at me quizzically. He had decided

that the app was not for him. He preferred to meet women accidentally, whatever that meant, and wherever that would happen. He had no idea of how much time I spent on it, of how much those random conversations continuously whirred in my head.

I already sensed that this digital discrepancy was pushing us away from one another. It was beginning to draw me into another world. I became addicted to the trepidation of waiting for one of my messages to be read, of imagining the effect it would have on its recipient as I turned the phone off when I went to bed. And waking up in the morning, I liked seeing messages on the screen and having to guess – since I could never remember their names, if it was from Arjan or Piet or Ivo who had, the night before, intrigued or provoked me, sent a clever question, liked a good film, or showed discernment in their taste in books. And then there were the signs on the screen indicating that the other was composing a message, those little dots appearing and disappearing as the person at the other end hesitated, stopped or started all over again. A strange disembodied intimacy emerged from typing up messages in black and white. In the absence of sound, touch, smell and taste, the small letters that appeared on the glowing screen each took on inflated potency as they channelled all emotions, thoughts and sensuality.

One day a texting maven caught me off guard. His messages had begun in the greyish hours of Sunday morning. He was an American expat who lived nearby. For a few hours as the morning settled in, we had shared our experience of being two foreigners living in the same corner of the city.

We teased and laughed and within hours, sexual innuendo turned into ways of baiting each other. His open questions felt like riddles, and our messaging turned increasingly suggestive, until it became clear that the situation required a kind of denouement that could not wait. At noon I was supposed to be making pancakes for the family. By two, having made the pancakes, I managed to leave the house, a cookbook under my arm and a confused story about needing to drop it off urgently at a friend's house.

Hopping on the bike, I was at his place within minutes, ringing the doorbell, and waiting with bated breath for him to open: this was ridiculous, exciting, absurd, dangerous perhaps. He opened the door, looked a little sheepish. A moment of awkwardness as I walked inside. The urgency of the world of the phone suddenly became what it has always been, a disembodied ersatz of the real thing. The teasing, sexually explicit guy who had made me feel restless and aroused all morning looked conventional to the core. He was muscular, tallish, with a strong jaw and brown eyes, dressed in faded jeans and a grey T-shirt. His ground-floor flat, newly renovated, was uniformly beige, in that particular tone that flats for expats are all decorated in. It was weirdly empty: half of the furniture had left along with his wife or was it a girlfriend two weeks before, he informed me as I looked at the half moved-in, half moved-out rooms.

He stood behind me and bent over to kiss me on the neck and wrap his hands over my breasts. I felt his erection immediately. He pinned me down on the sofa and, whispering some of those absurd lewd messages that we had exchanged a few hours earlier, told me how much they had turned him on. He undid his jeans and pulled out an erect penis, appearing to observe it with admiration. He did not fuss around with my clothes, but, penis in hand, asked me to show him my breasts. As I obliged, I realized that sex, for him, was all in the visuals. It was about cock, tits, ass and then, when I bent over the back of the leather sofa, it was all about positions: doggy style, missionary, spooning, cowgirl. A supersize saver box of condoms sat in the bedroom, on the single bedside table: less a full disclosure of his current lifestyle than a defence mechanism. He fucked by the book: the abridged version of the male narrative, from erection to ejaculation.

•

The quick tryst with the American expat had aroused me for all the wrong reasons. I returned home feeling both elated and sheepish, with the cookbook in hand and a made-up story up my sleeve. But Anton barely registered my presence. He and Victor were engrossed in building a huge ship from Kapla construction planks, after which Victor began to joy-fully dance around the fragile construction until, unable to resist, he kicked it and delighted in the sight of the patiently piled up planks collapsing in a second. I did not mention my little adventure to Anton that night or the days that followed, and he never asked about the cookery book.

The episode with the American expat had instilled a new kind of flippancy in my behaviour. I had walked into a fantasy this stranger and I had created together, and, immediately after the meeting, the dream had vanished altogether. I wanted to continue in that run, to take things as they came, decide on the spot: yes or no.

I began to seek out one encounter after the other more actively than I had until then. In the weeks that followed, the number of text conversations that led to coffees and then sex dates grew exponentially. I seemed to spend my time cycling across town from one date to the next, enjoying the idiosyncrasies of each individual and elated by the sex.

One of the first that month was a Dutch sound engineer named Felix with whom I spent an afternoon in the middle of February, on one of those few days when the city had been covered in snow. We had met in the café of the Rialto cinema near the Sarphatipark, and the sounds that came from there, of the kids shrieking with delight as they played in the snow, seemed to permeate our entire exchange. We both ordered cups of hot milk in which we drizzled honey and crumbled ginger biscuits as a kind of silly foreplay. He lived in the large house across the street which he shared with friends from the movie business and a black and white cat that meowed hello when we walked in. He caressed and licked and prodded me to tease out the orgasms that came in waves. He watched me writhe around on his bed and shout out my pleasure. He was not interested in classical intercourse but more into endlessly extending foreplay.

He didn't text me after that and neither did I. Instead, I struck up a conversation with someone called Väinö. Fresh from Helsinki, he had come to Amsterdam to intern in an architecture firm. I took him to Sauna Deco on a quiet evening in the middle of the week. He loved everything about the place, except for the temperature inside the sauna, which was far lower than Finnish standards, he sweetly explained to the bemused staff. He later reflected on the deep meaning of the Finnish sauna tradition. Hanging around in skimpy towels, we whispered dirty stories under the occasionally cross gaze of an old Dutch regular who pointed at the silence sign on the wall. The evening was so arousing that I did not need much more once we were alone, back in his tiny flat in the Jordaan. We were barely indoors than he proceeded to feel me up through my dress, pressing and squeezing my breasts. He then carefully nibbled, licked and kissed my ears until he triggered, quite unexpectedly, a full-fledged orgasm, which I experienced standing in his kitchen, fully clothed, legs shaking.

Both the sex and conversation had been thrilling and straightforward and we decided to meet again, but before that could happen, I went on a date with Stefan, a precocious German stage designer who dressed in hoodies and tweed jackets and explained he would be coming over regularly in the next few months to work on a theatre production. He had the pompousness of those who yearn to be taken seriously and told me of the salacious details of sex life in the German theatre world where polyamory was de rigueur. Sexually, he played it cool, but was really more gauche and nerdier than he let on. And yet he delivered. He was eager to please and happy to learn. His body was an enigma, large but light-footed; with a bouncy furry belly that gave him, when he lay down on his back, an unmistakable resemblance to Winnie the Pooh. He was the first German I had ever been to bed with and no matter what, that was never going to be a straightforward experience for someone from North London called Bloom. Back in Berlin, Stefan texted me regularly. He asked me about the 'Finnish intern', but a week later I had moved on to a journalist called Jonas.

Jonas was Dutch and mostly charming. After a late drink on the freezing terrace of Café Oslo, where we exchanged jokes while looking into the black water of the Sloterkade, snuggled on benches, wrapped in blankets, he invited me back to his place. Once there, he insisted on making out in the living room rather than in his bedroom and then pretended he could not remember where he kept his condoms. It took a lot of foreplay and convincing to get access to the bedroom and even more so to find the condoms that ended up being located, inexplicably, right at the back of a filing cabinet. There seemed to be a complicated story behind all of this that involved competing ex-wives and girlfriends. I did not want to hear about it. Despite all this, he was eager, and the chase around the house had only increased my determination to make him fuck me the exact way I wanted, on that very evening, even if his deviousness deterred me from wanting to contact him again.

'He isn't very straightforward in his journalism either,' Anton muttered when I told him about the adventure and the hidden condoms.

A few days after that episode someone called Arnold, with whom I had been chatting for a while, proposed to meet up in a bookstore, on a rainy spring day. He was fast-talking but elusive, half Dutch and half Indonesian. In his early thirties, like most of the others, he worked in PR and events. We met in a bookstore, and he wanted to know about the 'coolest' contemporary French writers. He was a fan of Houellebecq's latest novel, *La carte et le territoire*, which he had read in Dutch, to be sure to get all the nuances, he explained sweetly. I directed him to Virginie Despentes' *King Kong Theory*: essential reading for the emancipated man.

A few days later I joined Arnold at a trendy bar-restaurant on the top floor of a tall seventies modernist blue and grey brick of a building. It was the former headquarters of De Volkskrant newspaper, a landmark on the Wibautstraat, that motorway-like monstrosity that cut a permanent wound through the old neighbourhood at the east of the Amstel river. This was the place to be right now in Amsterdam, he said, wearing an inconspicuous uniform of blue jeans and matching shirt, turning his head away to invite me to observe the swarms of loud-talking, teeth-flashing, well-kept men and women besieging the bar. Beyond them, through the glass walls on both sides of the building, Amsterdam lay in the dark and thousands of twinkling lights. Arnold asked what art exhibitions were must-sees, the galleries worth checking out regularly, which local artists were 'hot', and what the standing of Amsterdam on the global art stage currently was. For all his posing, his lovemaking was impulsive, luminous, sensitive, emotional.

Several times that night I tried to tear away from the cave-like alcove in Arnold's studio flat where his bed was

concealed amidst piles of books. Half-dressed, I returned
to his embrace for more, and again, until I finally left in the
small hours of the morning. I cycled home, over the bridge
on the Amstel and through the deserted streets, under the
pouring rain, soaked and shivering in a dream-like trance. As
I arrived home, the purring of the refrigerator only emphasized the quiet darkness of the apartment.

Everything seemed so tidy, organized, unknown. I
padded into this house where everything seemed to have a
place, coats on a rack, a schoolbag on the floor near the door,
a tidy living room, with piles of books neatly stacked on low
tables. In the kitchen area, breakfast was laid out for three.
I stood there for a while in total silence. The water trickled
from my face and my clothes, as if I was still melting, dissolving into my own water, as I had done earlier in Arnold's
room. I was a stranger amidst these signs of a contained,
regular life, that looked as unfamiliar as if I had broken
into someone else's apartment. Eventually I found my way
to the bathroom where the scalding shower slowly brought
me back home. And then quietly, dry and clean, I slipped
between the sheets, tucked myself against Anton. I felt his
regular peaceful breathing, the warmth of his body. Desire
surged. I pressed my body closer against his, I ran my hand
smoothly across his chest, digging into the hairs with my
fingers. I felt the slight swelling of his belly; the relaxed muscles of his arms. I felt a deep comfort suddenly; being there,
peacefully with Anton. He grunted a little, turned around
in his sleep, and I felt his erect cock prodding against my
hand: a morning glory.

•

It was now properly spring, in that awkward week that separates March from April when rain showers alternate with sunny spells; and when looking up you can see the buds on the trees just about to bloom but hesitating still to do so. I examined them through the window of Odette's, the Ottolenghi-inspired eatery where my friend Cassie conducted her more casual work lunches, as I waited for her. Another shower. She'd probably sit that one out and join me after; her gallery was a good few hundred yards away.

She finally arrived, in her straggly-chic bob, fawn trench coat, masculine trousers and the just-released Raf Simons Stan Smiths, the uniform of the blue-chip gallerist between flights. Years earlier, Cassie's presence in Amsterdam had been a factor in my decision to move there, when Anton had asked me to, a few years into our relationship. She had come from the United States to study in London, and we had met during fresher's week at university. We had become steadfast friends, losing sight of each other and reuniting intermittently over the years as she followed a steady career in the gallery world in New York and London, while I lost myself in a PhD and tried my hand at teaching, museum curating and art criticism, starting and stopping a new career every few years. The opportunity to run the Amsterdam outpost of a well-known New York gallery had been a godsend, she'd said. She was one of those Americans with Dutch ancestry who loved the idea of returning to the motherland, the city that had given Manhattan its first name, New Amsterdam. It was the place where she was bound to end up, she told each new Dutch client and artist at the gallery explaining how she had fallen in love with the 'old' Amsterdam. Since I had arrived Cassie had been there for me, guiding me through the art scene and its networks.

'Oh my God, how ridiculous, all this flying!' she sighed as she slipped into the faux-leather banquette. This time it was three art fairs and countless meetings around them:

'Art L.A., ARCO Madrid and the big one in New York, the Armory show. I wasn't sorry to miss this weather, though.' The rain had begun to fall again. She pointed to the window with a little upward movement of her chin, simultaneously grabbing the menu to give it a brief glance.

'I'm having the shakshuka with eggs,' she declared, grabbing a tiny piece of bread from the French brasserie-type wired basket, and looking me up and down:

'Darling, I have missed you! And I haven't been running for ages, let's go soon. How's the thing going with the design museum? Did they ask you in the end?'

The sight of a waiter interrupted her flow of words. She waved him over.

'Oh, alstublieft, please, we're ready to order. What are you having, my love?'

'I was thinking, the warm lentil salad with salmon. And fresh ginger tea, please . . .'

'Oh, that tea sounds delicious! I would like that to drink with my shakshuka, please,' Cassie interrupted, smiling at the waiter. Her energy seemed limitless this morning.

I placed my elbows on the table and cupped my chin.

'OK, first tell me about your travels around the world.'

She drew her eyes towards the ceiling in a mock-exhausted look, and proceeded to tell me about the art fairs, the trade gossip, the parties, the clients to entertain, the general market trends.

'Lots of handmade stuff this year, it's like all artists suddenly discovered a kiln and a pottery club around the corner.'

'Or they've been reading Richard Sennett's book about craft. It still seems to be in fashion these days.'

'Really? Well in any case, this whole movement feels like a backlash against technology and its coldness. But it won't last, I am sure. Like everyone, artists are just engulfed in this new tech universe, with its smooth surfaces and the way it compresses our experience of the world, and trying to make sense of it. I think that will show in the coming years. It's bound to, anyway.'

I filled her in on the Design Museum exhibition project and David's unspoken wish that I would bring in some flashy artworks dealing with technology, by hip artists. I told her my apprehension about capitulating to the art market.

'But darling, you can't escape the market – that's a fact, and it would be absurd to do so – but it's not the devil. And I think David trusts you more than you think. He is also a more subtle thinker than you give him credit for. I think you basically have a "carte blanche" there. But I could of course suggest one or two artists when you tell me what direction you want to go in.'

We talked shop a while longer, then families – her teenage son was becoming increasingly tetchy with Marcus.

'Let's walk back to the gallery together and grab a cup of tea. It's Monday, terribly quiet. We can chat a bit more and we need to schedule some runs in the park.'

In between showers we walked down the Spiegelstraat, lined with antique shops that sold the dream of seventeenth-century Holland to moneyed visitors who came out of the Rijksmuseum, a few steps away. The gallery she worked for had settled in a nineteenth-century townhouse on the corner of the P.C. Hooftstraat, equal distance from high-end shopping and fine art museums. We made jasmine tea and settled into the deep sofas in the gallery's first-floor show-room, a high-ceilinged former reception room with elegant blackened parquet and pure white walls. It overlooked the busy Stadhouderskade with a view of the bridge that led to the Rijksmuseum. Sunny spells and showers continued to alternate with the exactitude of a delayed metronome as tourists, undeterred, stopped and took pictures on the bridge.

I finally told her about the dating app. We had confided in each other about our love lives and adventures since our student years. Cassie had always been a serial monogamist, her choices underpinned by an unshakable conviction that she would find the right man – or rather one right man for each different period of her life. In the past, we had spent hours and days unpicking love troubles, sharing doubts and joys, and now I described the app to her, the relentless rise of my libido and some of the brief adventures that I had had in the past weeks.

I spoke of the married Italian scientist, who, over our first coffee at café De Jaren, had whispered in confidence how much he would like to make love to me right now in the restrooms. He had come to visit at home when Anton was away at his parents' with Victor. He wore knee-length socks and perfectly starched striped shirts, and carried an Everlast sports duffel bag because he told his wife he was going to the gym when he came to visit. The perfect cover, he said. He was enthusiastic and, sexually, very dedicated. He just had no idea of how much he conjured the image of a spoilt, overgrown child, traipsing around with his sports bag and knee-high socks.

I told her about the Finnish architect, the Dutch sound engineer and the German stage director. About the Kenyan businessman and his electrifying touch, who later on in bed, had complained that I 'moved too much'. I spoke about Arnold, the PR guy, but I omitted the squeaky-clean, thrusting American, although she would have enjoyed that one, the kind of man she had wanted to escape when she had left the United States for Europe. I overlooked one or two more as I played up the entertaining details, the charming flaws, the funny anecdotes.

'This dating app thing basically feels like having unlimited access to the cookie jar,' I concluded, lightly. She laughed, then chided me gently.

'It sounds like a lot of fun, but when on earth do you find the time to see these guys? Aren't you juggling all these jobs and just got that exhibition commission, how are you managing all that at the same time?'

'I have never thought about it in that way, I don't know ...

these sex dates just seem to fit around my day. I meet them in between work meetings for a quick coffee, always in a place that I ask them to pick. That tells me a thing or two about who they are. And then, if there's chemistry, it just happens, then and there or another time. Time is elastic.'

'What do you mean?'

'Well, I don't spend my time in meetings or flying around the world as you do. And then those dates ... they energize me more than anything.'

'Really? Seriously, though, does Anton know? What's his take on this?'

'He is fine. These days, I've given up telling him about each and every one, there is no point. I mention them occasionally ... like this PR guy, Arnold. Turns out, he had applied for a job at the art school, some years back. I think Anton just knows that I am going through a phase and that it will pass. He is a bit like you, a serial monogamist. He was seeing this Colombian architect last winter, and I have a feeling there is someone new in Germany. But he hasn't told me about it yet. As long as things feel balanced between us, and we know where the other one is, that we are happy together, that Victor does not know a thing and feels we are there for him, it is all good.'

'But how many times do you meet each one?'

'Many of them only once or twice. They all have something interesting about them, but I have come to realize over time that what fascinates me about these guys is something else. I want to understand what their drive is, what their insecurities are about, how they make choices in life.' Amsterdam always was a city of entrepreneurs, I reminded Cassie, and so many of these young men had plans to set up a start-up of some kind. I liked to witness that carefree self-confidence and energy. And I enjoyed watching them navigate masculinity, in their behaviour as much as in their body. Some exercised a lot, others worried openly about their beer belly. And many of them shaved their bodies extensively: armpits, chest and genitals.

'Oops, TMI!' Cassie recoiled at the vision.

'Sorry.' I laughed. It seemed to be a generational thing, this shaving. I had read so many articles about the pressure on women to shave their pubis to stereotypes straight out of porn, that I had been shocked to see how widespread shaving was amidst men in their thirties. The sky was clearing up again. 'Sometimes I just want to tell them that it's going to get better, that there's an easy solution to the girlfriend-job-baby-house conundrum, but I don't want to sound like their mother. I am sure that if I meet any of them again, say in two or three years, they will all be pushing baby prams in the park.'

'I see exactly the type you are describing. They are young enough to wear their fragility on their sleeve. They must love to speak with you; older, wiser, knowing exactly what you want.'

'I don't know. Anyway, that's also why we don't meet more than a couple of times. We are all going places.' I grinned. 'At least they feel they are.'

'But wouldn't you like to have a full-blown affair, like Anton does? And aren't you afraid of falling in love?'

'No risk of that: there is no comparison between these guys and Anton! And I just love to meet these people who are open to sex without ties of any kind. Some have told me it's nice to go on a date and not to be asked about how many kids you want and how much you earn, for a change.'

'Seriously? Do women actually ask that?'

'Apparently some do, yes. And I just really like the surprise of the first encounter, the thrill of discovering a new body and all that.'

'So, you meet all these guys and you don't see them more than a few times each?'

'What's the point? The whole idea is that there is no past or future. There is only the present moment.' I shrugged and drained my cup of tea.

'It seems so . . . I don't know, cold-blooded, unromantic, so mechanical.'

'No, that's not it. It's pleasure at the touch of a button, it's magical.' Cassie should get this. She shared the abruptness of the Dutch and had a directness that served her well in her job in the country that she had made her home long ago.

'Remember,' she stretched back on the sofa, 'when we were together at uni and just afterwards, when we were still in London. All these love stories we would spend hours discussing. We made big plans, like each affair could be life-changing. We held these emergency meetings at the British Library when you were worried that your Japanese boyfriend would ask you to move to Tokyo, or when the Bulgarian guy suddenly imagined you would spend all your summers in Varna! We imagined entire lives shaped by our relationships:

each one opening a different path, a different life story. I
loved that.'

'And you have lived all these stories: a life in California,
another one in Paris where you had a baby, and now in
Amsterdam, with Marcus, who is such a great guy.'

Suddenly, looking at Cassie, I saw the determination and
the work behind the casual lightness she often affected.

'I also thought like that, back then,' I went on. 'I was fascinated by the idea of an entire world, a whole new life opening
up thanks to one person. But that was when we had no idea
what we would do with our lives, when we were students and
our plans were vague and limitless. I still am fascinated by
encounters in themselves. Now that I have no plans to change
husband or life, I can repeat over and again that moment of
the encounter, with a different man each time, one orgasm
leading to another.'

'But where's the utopia?'

'It's in that moment alone, the moment of the encounter:
I like the randomness of these meetings. These guys are
strangers with whom I share no friends, no acquaintances
or work colleagues, whose life I know almost nothing about.
They are the product of a computer algorithm filtered through
our intuition and then personal chemistry. Social pressure is
minimal, and I have discovered that out there, there are a lot
of people who are happy to have this simple, beautiful sexual
encounter, people who are incredibly good at sex, and who
don't mind having nothing more than a good conversation
next to that. So that's the utopia: the momentary drunkenness
of boundless sexual pleasure. It might occasionally trigger

infatuation, for a few days maybe, but one that bears no burden of responsibility to a narrative, a future. It's a utopia of the present moment.'

'What is it about, then, for you?

'It is about pleasure, lots of it, pure shared pleasure, with no accountability.'

'Anything else?'

'It's probably also, and this is connected to the accountability issue, about carving out pockets of time during which nobody knows where I am or what I am doing. Moments during which I am not beholden to anyone. Pockets of time stolen from the flow of productivity and efficiency that everyone else is engulfed in. Suddenly, for a few hours, between the four walls of a stranger's room, you can let go, step into a bubble that feels untouched by the exterior world, let your body and mind relax.'

'Is that it?'

'Well, maybe it is also about being shaken up by this otherness, by discovering a body that is not your own.'

'And?'

'When I come back home late at night after having been with someone, I cycle through Amsterdam and brush past the nightlife of the city. I see people coming out of bars, walking dogs, groups of people laughing drunkenly on the streets. Sometimes I feel like I could change course, and instead of coming home, go to another home and slip into one of several different beds occupied by men I have sex with. At those moments I feel I could possibly live different lives all at once, in the space of one night. Although it is an illusion, I feel I have now come to know more of the city's inhabitants and places. I know more bedrooms, more faces, more bodies. And all that gives me this vertiginous sensation that I am more intensely alive.'

Lucinda Childs, National Opera
& Ballet, 12 March 2014

Anton had booked the tickets.

'It's called *Dance*, by Lucinda Childs.'

'But I've already seen it,' I had replied. 'Twenty years ago, in London, dancers in gym shoes skipping around the stage.'

The sight had revolutionized my understanding of everything I thought dance was: scripted moves performed in tutus, glitter make-up and pointe shoes.

This time, though, it was the music that first captured my attention as it began to resonate through the theatre. A repetitive score, shifting layers of sound, waves that overlaid one another, from which a melody seeped through, an abstract, two-syllable tune.

In groups of four, dancers sprang from the wings. They skipped, jumped or even broke into runs across the stage, from left to right, from the back to the front. Now groups of two, similarly dressed in white leotards and wide-legged trousers – vintage tennis meets aerobics – appeared. They too energetically bounded across the stage, creating diagonal lines on the grid marked on the floor. At first imperceptibly and then visibly, the dancers moved in and out of sync with the music, the patterns of their steps becoming more compli- cated with each new sequence. Now they twirled as they ran, formed clusters that spiralled in and out.

The lights changed. A translucent screen became visible on the stage, showing a recording of the first performance of *Dance* in 1979, the one with Lucinda Childs.

For a while it seemed that the faded, greyish images of the film cast exact shadows on the dancers onstage, precisely mimicking their moves. And then suddenly the hypnotic synchronicity was shattered. Lucinda Child's face appeared on the screen, monumental and ghostly. She looked straight ahead, shoulders and arms turning to the left: a pirouette arrested in mid-motion now suspended in time.

The dancers in the theatre continued, meanwhile, to criss-cross the stage in groups of twos and fours, only now somewhat puppet-like, despite their relentless moving, skip- ping and gyrating. Nothing in the energy they displayed could match the intense, powerful liveliness of the screen image of Lucinda Childs, frozen in mid-motion. More than ever, as they jumped, regrouped and dispersed within the safe boundaries of the grid on the floor, they looked like marionettes kept alive by the incessant humming of the music, the waves of sound that ran parallel to one another, that overlapped and pulled apart.

6

Glitches

'What's going on, my love? You look tired, and you seem so restless. I feel like we haven't spoken properly for a while.'

Anton's voice, concerned, his tender gaze. We were at home together, a rare occurrence these days. For weeks we had been passing each other in the house like ghosts always heading in different directions: to Victor's school or picking him up from playdates, to studio visits, to meetings, public lectures, art openings, and then Anton had begun making short trips to Germany, to give lectures at the art academy in Düsseldorf. When we did speak, we exchanged to-do lists and reminders, usually about Victor, whose life continued, cheerful and undisturbed amidst these frantic, part-time parents.

With the warm weather slowly returning to the city, cafés began to open their terraces, not yet sprawling along canal-sides and over bridges but already beginning to give Amsterdam that hedonist atmosphere that I never felt in the same way back in London or Paris. Within a couple of months people would be riding on their bikes in flip-flops and tank tops, a rolled-up towel wedged under an arm, on their way to swim in the IJ from one of the designated piers or just any-where the water seemed clear enough for a quick dip.

But for now, it was the art scene that emerged from the quieter winter months. Exhibitions opened weekly in every gallery, artist-run space or museum. People were hungry to see art, to listen to public discussions, to see more of each other.

Some evenings Anton and I began together. After instruct-ing the babysitter, we would cycle to an opening in the Jordaan or de Pijp, or occasionally, in alternative spaces in up-and-coming neighbourhoods in the Nieuw-West or east of the city, by the Oosterpark. Once there we disappeared amidst groups of artists, curators, critics and museum people, a younger international crowd gradually outnumbering the Dutch old guard. We looked at art, we spoke and drank, and slowly parted ways. Anton was often invited for formal vernissage dinners where he thought it was important to 'show his face' and represent the art academy he ran, or to support a former art student on the verge of a breakthrough. I would linger for a while speaking with acquaintances on the sidewalk, amidst the increasingly animated crowds drinking beer and cheap wine. Later, when people began to make plans for the rest of the evening, I would slip away unnoticed and cycle across the city to join a stranger in a bar or an almost-stranger in his home.

Earlier that evening I had picked up a slightly dejected Victor from football practice. He'd scored an own goal and was mortified, the fine lines of his eyebrows creasing into a disconsolate frown:

'We won in the end, but still. It was soooo embarrassing.'
The perky self-confidence of my little boy was shaken. We
talked it through while waiting for his bath to run, and over
his dinner, as he brooded between mouthfuls. 'So embarrassing,' he repeatedly burst out. But later, perched on a bar stool
next to me in the kitchen, he seemed to have forgotten about
it all, as he did his homework, conscientiously filling in an
empty map of Dutch waterways and musing about places we
should visit together. I was never of much help, my Dutch still
floundering despite years of living in the country, but he sat
with me, occasionally glancing up inquisitively as he watched
me massage the kale with olive oil and chilli flakes.

I finished preparing a late dinner for Anton and me. Victor
went up to prepare his school bag. Left alone, I looked around
the sparsely furnished living room, dominated by the angled
sofa and a low elongated teak sideboard we had bought as
soon as we had decided to move in together. It had been far
too expensive for us, but as a statement of our desire for joint
home ownership, it came about as close as we could get.

The sideboard was by Cees Braakman, one of the designers
who had reinvented Dutch furniture after the Second World
War. I liked the idea that it combined the legacy of the Dutch
geometry of Rietveld and De Stijl with the modular design
of Charles and Ray Eames, whom Braakman had perhaps
visited in California when he was sent to study modern furniture in the United States. And then, for some reason, he had
called the series that our sideboard belonged to, identified by
its square receding black metal handles, the Japanese Series.
All this for the emerging Dutch middle class of the 1950s. A

compression of Dutch post-war sociology and design, with a bit of cold war geopolitics thrown in, stood in the living room.

It was usually covered with signs of our household's activities. Unopened mail sat next to brightly coloured stiff cards – invitations printed at great costs by museums and galleries to announce their exhibitions. They concealed lists of things to do, and not to forget, notes hastily scribbled on colourful sticky squares of paper, and left on the way out for the other to know, remember, to think about. A random sweatshirt found in Victor's school bag, the ownership of which eluded us for weeks, sat there too with Victor's iPad, sets of house keys, wallets and phones along with a book or two on their way from the bedroom to the study or from a bag to a shelf. It was a summary of our life throughout the week, before our ritual Sunday clear-up so that Monday could begin with a blank slate.

Now it was my turn to perch on the bar stool while Anton cleared up our dinner, having enjoyed the roasted kale and the salmon that I had confit in harissa oil. I observed each of his gestures, calm, efficient, precise, as he rolled up the sleeves of his improbably coloured coral pink jumper, gathered the dirty plates and washed the pans. He had once been a dishwasher in a restaurant, he liked to remind me.

As he soaped the oven dish, he inquired:

'I thought you wanted to meet men, and possibly women your own age, of your own generation and all that? But these are all guys you are telling me about, and they seem to be way younger, aren't they?'

I told him about the bulging necks and balding heads, the dearth of interesting-looking men in their forties. I explained how the women were few and far between on the app, and how that desire was so dormant now, that it was perhaps part of my long-gone student years.

'Those who write on the dating app that they are in their forties look way older, not sexy at all. And these guys in their thirties, they just seem to be free, more open to this.'

I told Anton about several of the men I had seen in the past few weeks. I seemed to be meeting 'a lot of different guys', he pointed out. Increasingly, I was less precise with numbers. I just shared the highlights. I told him about a freckled-faced graphic designer obsessed with the history of typography who played hard to get and about an accountant whose hobby was obstacle course running in the mud. Had he ever heard of that? I turned them into colourful, intriguing figures and said little more of substance. He didn't ask, he was game.

He told me about the end of his affair with the Colombian architect who lived in Rotterdam.

'It was beautiful at the beginning. Luciana's story, her passion, her desires. She is still married but her marriage is non-sexual, by mutual consent – apparently, that's a thing, nowadays – and so they have affairs they keep secret from one another. The husband is her partner in the architecture firm. But, after a few months, the spark just disappeared. I became bored with her conversation. With the sex, too. There is not much more to say.'

He looked at me thoughtfully.

'I'm sorry about Luciana.' I bit my lip. I remembered,

months back, scrolling through their messages when I had chanced upon Anton's unlocked phone. I had been jealous, rattled by the passionate tone of their conversation during the first months of their affair. He had never found out, I hoped.

'It's OK, part of the game. But I need you to be there, to stay close and not run away from me. That's one of the rules, right? We need to stay close to balance things out. You know I tried to explain this once to Floris, that we can be both intimate and yet also give each other that freedom. He said Adelia would never accept that.'

'I wonder if he ever asked her. Anyway, he might be right.'

'I still remember how you tried to sell me the idea at first, you were so ballsy, so rational about it. A flawless argument.' Anton gave me an ironic grin.

'Really? I think I was just reacting to your crazy principle that our marriage would last "forever". Your words. You gave me the security I craved and in return I asked for freedom. Straightforward enough, I suppose.'

'No, that was not it at all. You said that it made no sense to only sleep with each other for the next half-century that our marriage might conceivably last, don't you remember?'

I did. I had read out longevity statistics for women and men to him and said that if he was so certain that our love was forever and our marriage for good, then why should we not trust one another to have multiple lovers like we did before we got together? I had provoked him, he had laughed. And then, we had talked about it for weeks. We had outlined likelihoods and imagined situations. We had weighed up freedom against possessiveness, had forbidden

ourselves to be jealous, and talked with Anton's old friend
Sven, whose marriage to Tom had been open from day one,
and who seemed to be living happily together ever after. We
had agreed on the rules. And then, slowly, we had slipped
into that new life, seduced and been seduced, talked again,
changed the rules, confided in one another, altered the
rules again.

I pulled out a handful of crinkled, pale green verbena
leaves from the wide jar on the kitchen island and carefully
distributed them into two tea filters as Anton placed two
large glass mugs in front of me, a damp tea towel flung over
his shoulder.

'Star anise?' I asked, holding up the woody flower-shaped
spice, and rolling it between my fingers. I loved the glistening
dark eyes of the spice in their coarse woody casings. I popped
one in each mug without waiting for an answer.

'Talking about the age gap,' I started, hesitantly, 'I have
to tell you about something. The other day, I was speaking
with this Stefan guy I mentioned once. The one who works
in the theatre, the German guy. He told me he is trying for a
baby with his wife and it is provoking all sorts of existential
questions in their couple. His wife is an actor, early thirties,
like him, and they are afraid it will change their relationship,
independence, career plans, etc. He asked me for advice.'

Anton poured boiling water into the cups, adjusted the
filters and we walked over to the sofa.

'And what did you tell him? That you have an exceptional husband who does at least half of the housework and
child rearing?'

I huddled at one end of the couch.

'I did tell him all that,' I smiled vaguely, 'but I also went back in time and told him everything I had gone through, physically and psychologically, with the birth. Do you remember? How miserable I was at the end of the pregnancy and after Victor was born?'

'You had a *mild* depression, my love.'

I hated that phrase. I had been shocked by the transformations that pregnancy and motherhood had brought about. The woman who strode confidently down the street, who laughed when her skirt blew up in the wind as she rode her bike, the sharp-tongued critic who danced all night with smug artists and wild gallerists, seemed to have vanished in the eyes of others. She had become a mother, a figure simultaneously revered by society for putting out babies, but also pushed away from the world of seduction, the world of meaningless flirting. A whole lightness of being had disappeared from my life in the space of a few months as I pushed the buggy in the street, with the day's shopping in the basket underneath. I had felt invisible. As soon as I could I had propped Victor onto a little seat at the front of my bike. It had helped with the self-image, at least. I had explained all this to Stefan, how that had been the real trigger for the open marriage, that image of the transparent, shapeless, exhausted woman pushing a buggy around town. How essential it had been in helping me to find myself again and reconnect with the woman I had been. How I had needed to escape that box, the image of a woman whose body had become larger and softer through pregnancy, whose life now was inescapably connected to this cute baby. I had told Stefan how the first time I had flirted at a party and found myself kissing a stranger had helped me redefine the boundaries of my body and remember it could experience sensuousness. How that had helped me to rediscover the individuality of my being.

Anton sat at the other end of the sofa and caressed my stockinged legs. He stayed quiet, pensive, looking at me. I crawled up to his end of the sofa and curled into his arms. We made love that night, quietly, our bodies, used to each other, nesting naturally within each other's curves and limbs. And then we fell asleep on our designated sides of the bed.

●

The discussion with Stefan had pained me more than I had realized at first. The memories had torn back, still vivid. Everything had caught me by surprise when Victor was born. The changes in my body; the sagging breasts, the stretchmarks, the weight that refused to shift, the perineum that had to be retrained and the constant exhaustion that lasted for years. But there was more. That feeling of responsibility. Nobody told you beforehand that it would be so visceral, just as nobody said how they would look at you differently, decide for you what concerns and interests you, and what doesn't anymore. I remembered parties that people told me I would not want to attend. I remembered people constantly asking me where baby Victor was when they saw me alone at an opening. It was as if maternity had propelled me into another world, full of prams and nappies and conscientiously adhered-to timetables.

Perhaps that was also why I liked younger, childless men, men who carried on living the life I had stopped living when I turned thirty-four. However much I resisted the idea, I had to admit that I went to bed with a particular type of man: waifish, thin-boned, youthful-looking. They had no family of their own, were often in between serious relationships, or afraid to commit, or they were 'taking time to think'. The kind of man to avoid for a serious relationship, but I enjoyed them precisely for their unwillingness to settle, for the way they wouldn't call back or ask when the next time would be. For a few hours at a time, they took me to a world without children or family life. Their fickleness provided the perfect balance to the stability that ruled the rest of my life. So much so that whenever the stream of affairs paused for a week of family holidays, I grew impatient and the most minute things could exasperate me. I made love with Anton with a renewed possessiveness that he accepted; it felt at times as if I were holding on to him as onto a life raft. And at the same time, I needed to go my own way, to seek a perpetual excitement of the senses without which life seemed dull.

●

The Easter holidays were over. March rolled into April and leant towards May. I was dating relentlessly and occasionally my judgement became clouded. That was probably how I ended up in the newly built apartment of a cocky estate agent called Sander in the neighbourhood of Nieuw-West, on a grey April afternoon. Sander drove a candy-coloured Italian scooter and wore his slim-fit trousers rolled up to show his ankles, and bright white shirtsleeves pushed up to reveal tanned arms. He was surfing the high wave of Amsterdam's real-estate boom, and was sharp to the point of cynicism. I disliked almost everything about him, but something in that distaste aroused me, challenged me to provoke him, made me want to perform.

We'd barely shared a cup of coffee in one of the newest trendy bars on the sullen Sloterkade when I agreed to go back to his place, a small apartment located on the first floor of a block of flats on the Orteliusstraat, one of the identical-looking streets in the brown brick modernist maze that is Amsterdam West, off the Hoofdweg. I let him strip off my clothes down to a purple lace panties and bra, which I was evidently wearing to show off. I was in a rush to get what I wanted there and then, to feel that orgasm high that I had been missing the last few days.

I told him exactly what to do as I kissed him hungrily and then climbed on top of him, pressing his face inside me, and then slipping slowly down his body, kissing and nibbling at him until I sat over his cock, pushing him inside and out as I rose and fell at a measured pace. He cupped my breasts through the lace, squeezing the nipples out of the bra, and I watched him as he looked at me expectantly, attempting to read on my face the signs provoked by his being inside me. I rose and fell slowly, pressing his penis inside of me, lifting myself all the way up until he gasped when our bodies separated from one another completely, and then pushing myself all the way down, squeezing his torso between my thighs. And then I pushed down even further, his sex inside me,

swaying back and forth and from side to side to feel it everywhere deep inside. I closed my eyes to better sense the tremors
that commenced below my hips and travelled throughout my
body until, pricked in a thousand places, I was quivering and
screaming. Suddenly released from the tension, I collapsed
over his chest like a rag doll. He caressed my head, combing
through the dark curly mass of hair with widespread fingers,
pulling it away from my face into a ponytail.

'You are pretty good at this, it's so sexy to watch you come.'

After a short while, Sander began to move his hips up and
down suggestively, to get his bouncy toy going again, and
I resumed riding him, instructing him as to when he could
come, not earlier.

Later, as I was getting dressed while he watched me, still
lying on his bed, he had asked with an amused smile:

'So, tell me, what is it you like about younger guys?

I pulled my tights up under my skirt, looking away. 'What
do you mean? How old are you?'

He raised a hand up in defence: 'It's OK! I love
older women.'

'Older? What do you mean, older?' I buttoned my shirt and
picked up my cardigan.

'Well, you know, like you, mature, in their forties, who've
had babies.'

'What? So why is that, then?'

'They're not stuck up, like younger girls, and they don't
want babies.'

He jumped out of bed and came up to me, cupped one
breast in each hand, through the fabric of the shirt.

'They have these great soft breastfeeding tits; they know what they are doing. I love to date older women like you. You are the classic MILF fantasy!' He laughed and kissed the tip of my nose.

I scrambled to get the rest of my clothes together and left as fast as I could. Later on at home, as I peeled off my lurid underwear and got into the shower, I felt like an idiot. A MILF. Damn. That explained the swiftness of the whole thing. There had been no real chemistry but I had trusted Sander's attraction to me when I was basically nothing more to him than a walking stereotype, a tick on a list.

•

Sander was a hiccup, a small glitch in a well-established system, a bug in the otherwise smooth succession of matching, chatting, and, if the mood was right, ecstatic climax. It was as devoid of surprises as a set of moves across a board-game. Once the rules had been established, sex could take different forms and variations: closeness, a playful intimacy or a sexy mutual provocation. There could be speaking or silence; a variety of positions that all ended in climax. Equal parts strategy, luck and chance, that was how the boardgame worked. Like a choreography performed across a grid marked on the floor, it functioned smoothly as long as I followed the rules of the game and stayed within the limits of the board.

Within the boundaries of the board, I trusted my intuitions, I knew my desires, I sensed the needs of my body. When my breasts were tense at the end of my cycle, when my hips became eager to sway and lift and perform their little mating dance, I knew I needed sex to appease it.

One morning, on a whim, I cancelled a studio visit to an artist. I knew I would not be able to sit there patiently as he unfolded his vision, demanding admiration towards his masterpiece in the making and solicitude towards the throes of his creative process. Instead, heading out of the house under a low grey sky, I had texted a physiotherapist in training named Rutger, with whom I had had a drink a few nights before. He had the morning off so I cycled over to his place. The drink hadn't been bad, and I was feeling those little contractions in my belly I recognized as a craving for sex. It was like a wasp pressing its abdomen forward. I could feel the small, regular contractions of the body wanting to be touched. But once there, in his arms, the way Rutger touched and held me were all wrong. He was unable to read the map of my body, however much I guided him, and expressed in turn delight and annoyance as he squeezed and prodded different parts of me. I disengaged myself as quickly as I could. But it was impossible now to carry on with the day as if nothing had happened. The abdomen of the wasp was still pressing up and down increasingly urgently, in reflex. I texted Heiko who, uncharacteristically, answered straight away. By the time I had reached the ground floor of Rutger's building and unlocked my bike I knew where I was headed. Once there I knew I would get what I wanted.

I played with Heiko's body, explored it, gave him more than his usual reticence led him to accept. It was a powerful couple of hours: I came, squirted, came more. I was liquefying, melting. Water and shivers poured out, sending me into an oblivious, comatose bliss. After four or five meetings with him, I had become more straightforward and self-assured, and so the dynamics of our affair had changed. I was no longer passive and in awe of his magical hands. There was a new hardness in our lovemaking. It was not unpleasant but more demanding, like an old pair of lovers who know exactly which buttons to press but will make the other work a little harder for it. Maybe we had grown tired of each other, of the limitations of our exchange without admitting it.

When I left him to go to pick up Victor, a tightness surged unexpectedly in my chest, as I walked down the rickety staircase. I began to mourn what we had had. I was exhausted, hollowed out.

I manoeuvred as well as I could amidst the increasingly busy traffic. My reactions were too slow, I needed air. I resented the arrogant cyclists hooting impatiently at my clumsy reactions. I became fearful of the flow of bikes smoothly gliding around me. I no longer had the agility and wit to outsmart Amsterdam cyclists. I gave up when I saw the monumental elms of the Frederiksplein, parked and took a few steps past the circular fountain basin whose powerful, single jet dimmed the rumble of the traffic. I tried to breathe deep and slow to ease the lump in my throat. I dropped onto the nearest bench.

For a while I stared out, uncomprehending, at the fountain, the bushes, the flowerbeds, at passers-by who seemed to live in another world. I played over the events of the day: the mad cycling across the city from one place to another.

Back-to-back: two faces, two bodies, two homes in different parts of town. Two beds rolled around in, twice undressed and dressed again. My body, scattered across too many places, had gone through too many different states in too little time. Seduction, desire, frustration, letting go, being in control again. My only steadfast focus had been to reach another climax at any cost, with whoever was able to provide it. And now, rather than the sweet feeling of contentment, the self-assuredness and happiness that sex brought me, I felt anaesthetized, consumed.

I arrived at school late, and squeezed my way to the playground through clusters of chattering parents, mostly tall blond mothers in parkas and designer jeans who gave me a curt nod. Kids were running around wildly. There was no Victor amidst them. I spotted his friends and asked around, but they weren't sure. Maybe he was doing after-class duty, Guus's mother suggested in approximate English. I ran up the stairs to the classroom, but only found two other kids busy sweeping the floor and rearranging the tables. They looked puzzled as I breathlessly asked about Victor in my basic Dutch, then shook their heads. I ran back down, almost bumping into the assistant head. Calmly she checked records and reminded me that Victor was now, since the beginning of the term, allowed to go home by himself; if I couldn't see his bike in the racks by the entrance, he had probably done just that.

I rushed home, to find him sitting on the steps of our building, quietly munching on a croissant, his rucksack and jacket at his feet.

'I didn't have keys but Daan bought me a croissant at the bakery.' He waved the half-eaten pastry with a sweet smile, sending buttery flakes onto his lap.

I looked at his mop of chestnut hair and his skinny knees poking out of the oversize shorts he had recently taken to wearing.

'Can I have a bite of that?'

That night, I huddled into bed early, without waiting for Anton who was at a work dinner. I still felt jarred after missing Victor at school, after running around for him, after running around town from one lover to the next. I picked up my phone, briefly scrolled through the long list of matches and the conversations in progress and then pressed a button. Dozens of messages that might yield a few hours of pleasure in some bedroom across town, dozens of faces, of names and pictures disappeared in the space of a second.

●

When I awoke the next morning, bright daylight already flooded the bedroom. I lay still and attuned myself to the sounds of the house, expecting to hear the kettle burbling, the crockery clanking and the sleepy shuffle of Victor's feet across the wooden floor. But the only sound was the faint bustle coming from the street: Victor and Anton were gone.

I let the silence of the empty house envelop me, and felt between my legs. I patted the bulge of the pubis gently, caressed the short tuft of hair that was there. I thought again about the sense of dispersion I had experienced the day before, about my frenzied behaviour. But now I was there, complete again. I began to feel between the lips, to press at the flesh there. I caressed the little protruding button with my middle finger, patted it gently. The clit came alive, the familiar sensations began to run through my flesh, comforting, reassuring. I could give to my body what I looked for in other bedrooms, with other hands than my own. I stroked it gently and felt the tingling warmth, the wetness of the vulva, the slight spasmodic movements of the vagina coming to life, the contractions of the belly opening and closing. I rubbed faster around the opening of the vulva and felt the pleasure surge and seep through my flesh.

I must have fallen asleep again. When I awoke it was close to noon. I tiptoed downstairs in the empty house. I imagined myself another person, an entity referred to as a single woman. No imposed schedule, no need to be there for anyone, no need to be lively, upbeat and caring. A weight ordinarily ignored now, almost surreptitiously, lifted from my shoulders. I needed to take time off, to slow down, to think clearly. I could not believe the absurdity of that rushing between lovers the day before, as if climaxing was something I was owed, and then missing Victor, acting stupidly at school. I had lost a sense of perspective, had not been thinking ahead and erecting self-preserving borders. In the kitchen I found a note waiting for me on the island.

'Hope you are OK. Remember we love you.'

●

'Perhaps it is good you are taking a break,' Anton cautiously replied when I told him, that evening, that I had stopped using the dating app. He moved around the kitchen, collecting plates and glasses for the dishwasher, choosing his words carefully:

'I don't want to pry. But I have seen you looking paler, storming out of the house sometimes, like you don't want to be with Victor and me.'

'Has Victor said anything?'

'Not really; only that we were both going out a lot these days. But I was wondering if perhaps you were not just burning through these affairs?'

I had nothing to answer to this. Like a caged animal futilely looking for a way out. Burning through.

'Burning? What is that supposed to mean? These encounters are made to be short, there's nothing more to them than sexual adventure, and there would be no point in letting them drag on for weeks. I don't understand your way of doing it, these long-term affairs that follow one another. Maybe you should tell me more about how that works. Who are you seeing? Now the architect is out of the picture, what is going on in Germany?'

Ignoring the abruptness of my answer, Anton told me. He had enjoyed flirtatious conversations with several women in the past months, but nothing had happened for a while. Now he had a new lover, a Turkish-German painter who lived in Düsseldorf where he had been travelling regularly. They had met in a bar one evening after one of his talks.

'I feel more anonymous over there, in Germany, than here, and when I go, I hang out with this woman, Defne. I slowly immerse myself into the Düsseldorf art scene. I like that there is a strong underground cultural scene over there, one that still believes in the oppositional nature of culture in one of Germany's wealthiest cities. I like the country. And Defne, she is in her late forties, she drinks beer, she is a really good artist and she has this swagger.'

'A swagger? Sounds promising. Defne's a nice name. Tell me more. What does she look like?'

'She is a little boyish-looking, with black hair and a pixie cut, and we don't need to see each other all that often. I stay a little longer when I have to go to give those lectures, and we catch up, I dip into her world, for a day or two.'

'How does that work for you?'

'Like for you, darling, she is a respite from the "system", the household, the school hours, Victor's extracurricular activities, and playdates. And also, from the art school. I do so much admin over here that I enjoy, when I am with her, reconnecting with the process of making art. I spend time in her studio. I watch her paint sometimes; we talk about her work a lot. It feels good to be close to the intimacy of creating. That has become so distant in my everyday work. Just as you do, I think, I like stepping into a different world when I go there. And Defne somehow reassures me. I had been feeling like after fifty, no woman was looking at me anymore.'

•

In the first few days after deleting the app, my frustration grew. I tried to take things out on Anton but he told me to stop. I was acting ridiculous, even in the state of confusion I was in. We were going about the open relationship in different ways, but our motivations, our desires were similar. It was a thing we shared, and that should bring us together. We continued the conversation the following evenings. I wanted to know more about Defne and her work, her paintings of the sexual parts of men and women. She was inspired by Courbet's *Origin of the World*, and she read French psychoanalysis, currently Gérard Pommier's book on the meaning of 'making love', *Que veut dire faire l'amour?* He was reading it too.

'Things take their time to be lived out,' he mused.

'Things take their time to be lived out . . . It is a nice way of saying it . . . I am not sure if it really works that way, though.'

I was making dinner when the doorbell rang. Victor was being carpooled home with his friend Casper from a museum excursion with his drawing class. I pressed the intercom button to let them in.

'Can you get the door, please? Casper's dad is bringing the kids home – I've never met him.'

The boys clambered up the stairs jostling and laughing. I heard Anton get the door, and a voice echoed in the hallway. The two men were exchanging pleasantries. I knew it but could not place it and discretely padded towards the entrance.

'Gabrielle, this is Casper's father, Jonas!' Anton gestured to me to approach.

'Hi, hi,' I said, walking cautiously towards the man whose face was obscured in the shadow of the doorway.

'Thanks for bringing Victor home. Nice to meet you.' I looked up, took a detached air, and blushed violently.

The man on my doorstep was the charming and

complicated journalist who stored his condoms at the bottom of his filing cabinet.

Jonas stared at me for an instant, speechless, then mechanically proceeded to repeat the report he'd given to Anton about the tournament. I excused myself swiftly and retreated to the kitchen and let the two men continue to discuss our kids' achievements.

A text message vibrated its way onto my phone later that night:

'Such a surprise to see you, Ada, or rather "Gabrielle". Glad to learn your real name, by the way! Perhaps we should meet again? Genuinely sorry about the condom misunderstanding. Please call me.'

●

I did not call Jonas back. Or anyone else for that matter. In the weeks that followed, I spent most of my evenings at home, or went out with Anton. I read about the platform economy for the project at the Design Museum, I went to see exhibitions. I made the rounds of artists finalising applications; prepared files to review after the deadline, kept my co-workers at the foundation happy. I went running with Cassie and made dinner for Floris and Adelia.

On one of our evenings together they spoke excitedly about a small wood cabin they were purchasing with a group of friends outside Amsterdam, to start growing vegetables. They explained passionately how local, circular economies work, and told us stories about ancient vegetable varieties discarded by the ultra-intensive Dutch agriculture system.

'The system that works with these crazy gigantic greenhouses which you see from the motorway, fully lit up at night.' Their enthusiasm had a slight moralising tinge to it. Anton provoked them a little, to see how far their conversion had really gone. I was glad the vegetables I served that night were at least organic and reasonably local.

We also went to the movies as often as we could get last-minute babysitting from our neighbours, mistrusting each other's taste beforehand, and often debating after, the whole way home. At times we went with friends, to widen the conversation.

That night we'd gone with Cassie and Marcus to see Jonathan Glazer's *Under the Skin*, which Anton had picked.

'Do you remember, Gabrielle,' Cassie began to ask, turning around to face me as we stepped out of the cinema.

'... Do you remember that art installation in the old Saatchi gallery on Boundary Road?'

'London years,' I commented.

'We used to go there all the time, to the Saatchi, when we were students. There was this mesmerising installation at the top of the stairs, maybe a room under the roof. I think it had sloping walls. Anyway, it had a tank full of oil, completely black, that reflected the whole room, do you remember that piece? You would walk between the oil tanks in a narrow corridor and at the end, have this amazing impression it was all around you? I mean, don't you think Glazer must have seen it? It is so much like the black pool in the movie.'

We were walking home together, and after skirting the Leidseplein packed with tourists filling the café terraces, we stepped into the Vondelpark. The air was distinctly cooler under the trees that lined the bike path.

'What was the name of the artist? Not Robert Wilson?' I remembered repeated visits to that installation. I would climb the stairs up to the quiet gallery at the top, and walk through the narrow opening until I was surrounded, from the waist up, by this oily reflective deep black surface. It gave me an eerie feeling of weightlessness, of time and space suspended.

'Richard Wilson, yes, that's it,' Cassie strode on, a jubilant note in her voice, 'and that work came back to me in those scenes where Johansson urges the men to join her in that murky fluid. There was that similar sense of alienness. And the sound in that scene was also incredible.'

'What impressed me most,' started Marcus, 'was that guy on a motorcycle . . .'

'Yes, now what was that about? Johansson's superego?'

'More like some kind of guardian or supervisor of some sort? I don't know. Cassie, what do you think? Anyway, I wonder how they filmed those scenes. It's a pretty challenging drive, all those hairpin turns in the hills above the lochs, in that terrible Scottish weather. You would have to be a real pro to be able to drive like that in those conditions.'

Anton was transfixed by Scarlett Johansson's character and the mercilessness with which she picked up random men. I could not push away the final scene of the film, when she shed her skin. A malfunctioning alien machine, she got trapped in her own game, she was cornered. At the end, her human skin, the rosy soft skin of Scarlett Johansson – a brilliant casting choice – lay lifeless like a body suit, abandoned in the woods, set on fire. Only a shapeless black mass emerged. It was a striking image about what we are made of inside, a mesmerising vanitas about the perishability of the corporeal envelope. We parted ways with Marcus and Cassie in the middle of the park and walked arm in arm the last stretch of the way home.

The quiet obsession of Johansson's character, out on a mysterious mission driving around in her van, picking up men, was a powerful image that made an unspecified anxiety suddenly surface again. The absence of justification for her actions and the way she pressed forward, out of control, into the unknown, was fascinating.

Unable to sleep, I went downstairs and stretched out across the sofa in the living room. The flashes of light and the hissing sounds of the garbage trucks, the muffled noise of traffic at dawn brought up more images of the film. On the coffee table was Simone de Beauvoir's *The Second Sex*. Anton had left the book open. It was amazing, he had told me the night before, even just the beginning, the chapter about the amoebae. I wondered if that was also recommended reading from Defne.

I found my phone, kept on purpose as far away as possible from my bed. The small black rectangle shone in the semi-darkness, taunting me after weeks of abstinence and playing the monogamy game.

'Welcome back', said the app. 'Do you want to be visible again?' I acquiesced and a deck of cards manipulated by an invisible nimble-fingered croupier began to whirl from the depths of the phone towards the surface, landing perfectly flush with the screen. The first card appeared, face up, the deck ready for me to resume my exploration of available individuals within a seven-kilometre radius. I began to swipe, slowly and then faster. I recognized faces I had matched with before, chatted with, then discarded. I was on familiar ground, familiar enough to want to play and take risks. I had missed this buzz and was eager to return to it. This time, I might try to take it slow. Hours later, the phone whirred. Stefan, the German stage director, was in town for a few days.

PART TWO

7

Speculative Evaluation

The car picked up speed on the slip road and merged into the light mid-afternoon traffic on the motorway, leaving Amsterdam behind. I lowered the car window and felt the cool air brush against my skin.

'Today is Monday 16 June, why is this such a special day to you?

'If I tell you, I will give it all away. Let me keep it a surprise. It's a very special place. You will see.'

'Can you at least tell me where we are headed? A rough direction? North? West? South ... ?'

'South ... ish.'

'OK ... thank you ... So, how about a name of a place, so I can tell Anton when I call him in a minute? It's only fair I tell him what I am up to.'

'Hmm ... You can tell him you are going somewhere near Abcoude.'

I turned towards the man behind the wheel and shrugged:

'Abcoude? Never heard of it.'

A mischievous smile greeted my words.

'Don't be so impatient, you will see ... I have not been there for years, but I think it is still the same as I remember it.'

He glanced at the rear-view mirror as he spoke and I looked at the strawberry blond hair fluttering about in the car, the high forehead, pointed nose and round chin, and thought again about what had struck me when I had first seen Emil's picture on the dating app. I had liked the strange hair colour and freckled face, the delicate hands holding an opened book as he stood amidst what looked like printing presses.

'It was taken at the printing studio of Rob Stolk, the legend-ary Amsterdam printer and activist,' he had explained. 'Do you know the name? He was a crucial figure in the countercul-ture of the sixties, the Provo movement. Amsterdam legend.'

Emil kept his eyes on the road, looking for something.

The exit sign for Abcoude appeared. He drove right past.

'I have always loathed surprises, you know,' I said quietly, raising my eyebrows.

He smiled, looking straight ahead. Of course, I had accepted to go along with this in the first place, and there was nothing much I could do about it now. In truth, this excursion out of town followed on so naturally from the oddness that had characterized our affair from the very beginning that I decided to let go and stared down at the canvas bag wedged between my legs. It contained the rudimentary picnic I had put together in a few minutes after he had called, excitedly asking if I was free and if he could take me somewhere spe-cial, today. It had to be today, and did I have a few things we could take with us to eat on a picnic?

For our first encounter, at the beginning of May, he had

insisted on going to an experimental electronic music concert, rather than the customary coffee. I had stoically endured the performance, telling myself it was good to get out of my comfort zone, but hating it all along. I think he saw right through me then. I had felt a tension, rather than an immediate attraction, sitting next to him in the dark, looking at his profile as he focused on the music, eyes on the stern woman dressed in black, who sat at a table pulling jacks in and out of an old synthesizer and adjusting dials and levers on a giant mixing board drowned in a pool of cables.

After the concert he had declined to go and have a drink, but had agreed to a short walk. He was exactly my age, divorced and a part-time parent to a teenage daughter. He was a graphic designer, and in his profile photo he was holding his latest book project amidst printing presses, he explained. He told me extensively about his obsession with the history of typography, which he channelled into creating visual identities for companies and museums.

I wondered if on that first evening together he had felt my efforts to repress a promiscuousness that somewhat remained on automatic, like a default setting. I did not press on this time or the one after, and neither did he; he was present yet elusive. We met several times over a fortnight, for a quick lunch or to see an exhibition, and then he would disappear without any suggestion to go back to his place. I trod lightly, unsure of what this was turning into, unable to rush things and equally unable to cut him off.

Eventually came a moment when the cat and mouse game had been played for long enough, and he invited me back to his place for dinner on an evening when his daughter was away.

He took me through his collection of vintage letterpress printing blocks. 'As obsolete as they may look, the shape of letters still has a huge impact on how and what we think about the words we read,' he said, sententiously.

He took me through the history of typography and commented on how it had always been used, historically, to influence thought and alter the subliminal message conveyed by words.

'Today, even more in the age of digital technology and words on screens, it has an impact on the extent to which you trust a website or believe a political slogan.'

He took me through his collection of favourite books, pointing out the print quality and the particular typesetting of each one.

Finally, he took me through to his bedroom. In the weeks that followed, Emil inserted himself seamlessly into my life. We texted several times each day. He sent me inspiring quotes, songs that, he said, conjured an image of me when he listened to them, recipes for exquisite dishes and links to thought-provoking articles. I became used to the early morning whirr of the phone that announced his daily greetings, each morning a new message that caught the mood of the moment. I became attuned to his daily rhythm, aware of his timetables and to-do lists. I stopped using the dating app. At first, I still occasionally met with Stefan when he came over from Berlin, and sometimes with Väinö, the Finnish architect in training whose uncomplicatedness

I enjoyed. And then I saw them less and less and then hardly anymore.

After a while the narrow road turned into a dirt path that led to a farm. Emil parked the car. We walked past a couple of barns and stables. The place looked deserted. Without addressing me with so much as a word, he called out and eventually a farmer in jeans and rubber boots appeared. Emil exchanged a few words with her, and we followed the woman to an open hangar by a waterway. A pier came into view. It stretched some fifteen meters alongside the water, a dozen small faded red and green rowing boats moored to it. More talking, a couple of banknotes were exchanged and Emil joined me on the pier vaguely pointing at the boats.

'We can take any one of these, and need to bring it back at 9 p.m. at the latest.'

Emil manoeuvred away from the other boats and, following the directions given by the farmer, took a left into a narrow waterway, wide enough for a couple of rowboats at most. The water was a dark greyish blue dotted with small white waterlilies, and we glided slowly in between hedges of reeds and grasses that obscured the banks and cast shadows into the water. The hangar disappeared and an eerie silence settled in, hardly perturbed by the regular splash of the oars lifting out of the water and the dragonflies swishing by.

We progressed in silence through the waterway amidst the lush bushes closing in on us on all sides, the view almost identical at each turn. Suddenly, the waterway opened onto a wide expanse of blue water glittering under the sun, a lake that spread out as far as I could see. Rugged edges framed the pool of water on all sides, forming strips of land covered in abundant grasses and cattails, and larger shrubs in the background. Everywhere around, basking in the exceptional heat of the afternoon, under a cloudless sky, ribbons of glittery water seeped through the greenery, a dark blueish liquid running through the jagged shores. A forest of semi-immersed aquatic plants quivered in the translucent water around the boat. There were delicately coiling feathery ferns in soft yellowish green, wide oval tender green papery leaves, spiky underwater grasses showing little more than their pointed tips. Green merged into blue that bled into the green. I had never seen anything like this place.

Emil stopped rowing as we reached the middle of the lake. We slowly took in the quiet, perfect beauty that surrounded us. He looked radiant.

'My parents used to take me here as a kid, with my younger brother. We came many times but I have not been for perhaps twenty years or so. It's called the Botshol.'

'What is it? A former polder of some kind?'

'Not exactly, but we are under sea level. It's a part of what is called the Vinkeveense Plassen. Basically, it is a series of interconnected pools and waterways, surrounded by marshes. It's a nature reserve now, but it used to be a peat bog. They started digging in the seventeenth century, mainly to use the peat for fuel, in Amsterdam. They dried the peat on those narrow strips of land which were all that remained above water when the digging caused the place to be submerged. And then more recently, they came here to dig out the sand to build the A2 motorway, the one we drove down on, so the waters in some of the pools are very deep.'

'And then, in a typically Dutch way, when the destruction of nature was almost complete, they turned it into a nature reserve,' I commented. 'I think I am beginning to understand, finally, how this country works.'

'That's exactly it,' he replied thoughtfully. 'It's so weird to see how human damage can then turn things into a place so peaceful, so beautiful. The kind of place that only appears in your dreams; the brilliance of the colours, the peacefulness. We are totally alone – between land and water, basking in the sun.'

'How did you know where to rent the boat?'

'The Botshol is a hamlet, with just a few farmers around, and two of them rent a few boats. It seems haphazard, but it's totally regulated. Only those boats are allowed on the waters, and they open every year on June 16 for the summer season. That's why I wanted to come today.' He looked all around at the shiny dark blue water.

'Come, let's swim!'

Emil began undressing on the boat, causing it to sway perilously from side to side. I did not have swimming things with me; besides, the water would be freezing.

He brushed my excuses away, he hadn't wanted me to know where we were going, but we were completely alone here, he assured me. We could swim naked. Emil had shed his clothes entirely and stood on the boat, his slim freckled body and rust-coloured hair contrasting against the matching blues of sky and water.

'Come!' He climbed out of the boat and splashed into the water.

Jumping ship sounded like a particularly bad idea to me. The possibilities of getting a heart attack from the cold water, the boat that might drift away, the sea creatures that were bound to be lurking around waiting for us as a treat. Emil laughed. I was such a city girl.

I removed my T-shirt and long skirt, and stretched out on the boat, letting the sun caress the exposed flesh. I slowly peeled off my underwear. Emil swam further into the lake. I slowly, clumsily clambered out, sensing the hard edge of the boat catching and cutting into my thighs as I flipped my weight and eased myself slowly into the cool water. The cold liquid licked my skin and I gasped as it trickled between my thighs. I slid further, lowered my hips into the cold water. I let go of the boat and let out a scream as the tip of my feet touched the soft, muddy bottom of the lake. I had never swum in fresh water before. Emil came back towards the boat and we swam out together, keeping our bodies as parallel to the surface as we could to bathe in the warmer patches of water. All around us the strong rays of sun pierced through the lake's trembling surface, creating light shafts that tunnelled into its depths. Further away the rays of the sun bounced off the surface, causing it to sparkle and shimmer, and the dense bushes of reeds on the banks took on an even brighter shade of green.

We clambered back onto the small boat after a while and rowed over to a short strip of land nearby, a miniature peninsula where we finished drying off and lay onto the grass. I felt the sun slowly erase the cold from my limbs and shroud them in a comfortable warmth. I gazed at the infinite cloudless sky as Emil nuzzled my neck and wrapped his body around mine.

We lay still.

A group of inquisitive ducks surrounded the boat; a heron stood on a grassy bank across a narrower stretch of water. We walked around the strip of land, naked. I asked Emil to tell me the names of the plants in the water around us.

'Water soldiers': he pointed at the green spikes barely emerging, crown-like. 'And these yellow flowers here, bladderworts, carnivorous plants.'

Small insects buzzed around; the rough grasses tickled my feet.

We spent the rest of the afternoon rowing across the lake, passing through waterways small and wide, dipping into the water, kissing and fondling on the grass, looking at the small white waterlilies unfolding their leaves on the quiet surface of the pool. We never saw another boat. The light became bluer as we feasted on tins of smoked mackerel and sardines, dunking chunks of bread in the oil, and a few apples and cherries washed down with sparkling water.

On the way back to Amsterdam in the car I asked if he had ever taken Sofija, this woman he had recently begun to see, to Botshol.

'No. I didn't think she would understand the place, that she would like it the way you would, and did.'

I asked him to tell me about her. I only knew her from a distance, a striking woman who worked in the art world.

He described her small but heavy breasts, her tightness inside, her golden skin and black hair. 'For her it is a triumph when she has an orgasm, but with you, your body seems so sensitive and it stirs in so many places. It's a completely different vibe.'

'I like to know about her. You must promise you will always tell me these things if I ask, be honest and transparent. That's how I do things. Total freedom and complete honesty.'

He promised.

Back at Emil's house, limbs still numbed by the cold water, and stiffened by the car ride, feeling a little dizzy from the heat, the light and the wind, we fell into his bed for a nap, snuggling up in each other's arms. When we awoke from slumber, it was dark outside, a moonless evening. We kissed and nuzzled, lazily teasing one another until we were both awake and aroused.

Sex with Emil had a special quality of slowness. It resembled a stroll that we took, each in turn, across one another's bodies. We explored the other's flesh as if it were a treasure map, discovering erogenous zones in unexpected places. Caressing, touching, nibbling, we observed reactions: shivers of pleasure, tingles of irritation or pain, murmurs of delight. We strove to define the geographic extent of each other's most sensitive territories, like ever-shifting continents, the maps of which we drew with inquisitive fingers running against smooth, moistening skin.

Pushing the covers back, he started feeling between my legs, slipping downwards to my inner thigh with a light touch that made me tremble. He took note of the tension there, and moved towards the knee. No quivering on the sides, here or there, but a light stroke across the fold at the back of the knee made me stir and so did the contact of his tongue as it licked the kneecap in sharp, brief, cat-like licks. He moved upwards again, taking in other areas of my body. He looked at the pearls of sweat that formed in the small of my back, felt again the slipperiness of my vulva, the hardening of the nipples as I held my breath. He pressed a moistened thumb into my ass and I pushed his penis inside it. I quivered. I pushed him out, back in again. He reached out with his fingers and slid them into my cunt. Like a doubting Thomas, he wanted to feel himself inside me. I wanted him to be everywhere at once. I pushed him out and back in, pressed him in turns into my cunt, my ass, my cunt again. I pushed him deep into my throat to mute the spasms shaking my body so the effect would be stronger.

I liked him to lie on top of me after sex, bringing his body perfectly into line over mine as I sunk, belly-down, into the mattress. His legs on my legs, his feet on my feet, arms and hands aligned exactly over one another. His weight distributed evenly on mine was barely perceptible, and I felt every tremor of his body as he breathed. In those moments we became one, exact doubles of each other. We imprinted the shape of our bodies on the other as we drifted away in the haze that follows coming.

I returned home late in the night, eyes still full of the grasses bristling in the wind above the ultramarine water, still feeling Emil's body wrapped around me like a shadow of my own. I walked around the moonlit apartment, made a cup of tea, unable to go to bed quite yet. Slowly, the images of the afternoon began to blend with a much older picture that they called up, a picture long forgotten that had seemed, when I had first seen it decades ago, a perfect representation of that watery freshness. A lush, green place that I had visited in my dreams many times.

In the semi-darkness of the living room, I turned to the bookcase and let my eyes slowly follow the spines of art books lining the lower shelves. I stopped at a thick heavy volume encased in a blood-red glossy dust jacket. I had received it as a going-away present at the end of my first summer job in an art bookstore. The spine read 'Robert Motherwell', spelt out in a reassuringly serifed black font. He was a second-generation American Abstract Expressionist painter. I leafed through the book, and found it: a painting that I had lived with for years in my head and yearned to see one day in real life. *Riverrun*, 1972. It was one of Motherwell's very large ones, almost four meters wide, a low horizontal format, reproduced in a fold-out in the book. At first, the painting seemed to be just a blue monochrome, painted patchily so that it appeared to be made of different shades of indigo, cornflower, steel blue, azure and lavender, a tint seeping into the canvas, in those places where the colour looked fluid and watery, rather than like paint layered on the surface. And then when you looked more closely at the image in the book, the blue shifted, or more precisely, it bled into patches of green shaped into wide diagonal strips, a fragment of a reversed 'w', painted in a softened blueish apple-green. And right there in the top right part of the picture was a portion of the painting I had forgotten all about.

It was a small black motif lightly sketched into the blue and surrounded with a foamy white blur. After this afternoon, I was now able to understand what it was, to read it as the stern of a small rowing boat progressing in a cool, lush watery blue and green landscape.

●

The exam season was nearing and Anton seemed to be caught up in endless meetings, reviews and supervising the summer exhibition of the Art Academy. Every time that he was held up by some event or another, I would ask Emil to join me somewhere. We went together to visit exhibitions and museums, he joined me at openings, and even sometimes at dinner with friends. Cassie and Marcus seemed to accept him. Emil knew her a little. He had once designed an exhibition catalogue for her gallery.

The small pockets of time that, only several months earlier, I struggled to tear out from everyday life to spend a few hours with a lover, now expanded both in time and space until life with Emil became almost a double of my life with Anton. Some evenings we cooked dinner at his place, then made love, before I returned home. Other times I joined him for a late breakfast, after Victor and Anton had left the house. We started the day afresh, as if there was another life that we could build together.

Gradually I started referring to him as my lover, rather than as a random 'date', one of many, faceless, nameless others. I began to toy with the idea of a polyamorous relationship. I read about shared digital calendars and the ethics of polyamory. When we were apart, I was with Anton and Victor, he was with Sofija. It all seemed perfectly balanced somehow.

Sex was always tender, sweet, joyful. Pleasure was more interiorized, untheatrical, than with the short encounters of the previous winter and spring. Emil did not have the eagerness I remembered in others, the famished excitement of sex between strangers who know they might not meet again and who want everything, immediately. Emil would walk around his house casually discarding his clothes one by one on the floor, each item in a different room, as if he was just changing outfits, chatting about things entirely unconnected as he did so. And then without warning, he would nonchalantly stumble into his bed, asking if I might agree to join him for a little nap. Not for sex, of course, just to be cosy, he would say. He had no interest in undressing me. It was up to me to take my clothes off under his amused gaze and slip into the bed, where he then proceeded to embrace me, run his fingers through my hair and feel between my legs. And then he would exclaim, every time as if it was a surprise: 'Oh, you are so wet down there!' And then the lovemaking began, slow, playful, tender, intimate, like teenagers doing everything for the first time.

When we did not meet for a few days, there were the multiple daily messages, and we spoke on the phone, sometimes for hours, other times just to check in. He lived on the edges of the art world and was curious about everything; he wanted to know about people, what I thought about certain artists, about the exhibition program of the Stedelijk museum, about networks of individuals and of ideas, and past artistic movements. He wanted my opinion about the most recent contemporary art display at W139 and at De Appel.

When the days became reliably warm, we went to swim together in open water, in the IJ. Emil introduced me to a swimming culture in Amsterdam that Anton did not care much for, and I began noticing the many small ladders leading down into the water, fixed on wooden piers and on the sides of stone riverbanks all across the city. Together, they turned Amsterdam into a giant swimming pool, freely available at any time of day and night. Some rumoured the water could make you sick, others brushed it away and went in every day. Nobody spoke of the vast network of cables down below in the depths of the sea, the Amsterdam Internet Exchange that Akwasi had described, dormant sea monsters that controlled and made possible all our online activities. Did they stop at the coast, or were they right there, under our feet, somewhere in the IJ? We swam at the Borneokade, where we ran into wrinkly Amsterdammers in jelly shoes, flowery rubber caps and worn-out swimsuits. We swam by the KNSM island where groups of teenagers squealed and laughed as they jumped in the water and raced to distant pontoons made of wood and steel, remains of the harbour's industrial activity. I longed to return to the Botshol, for us to be alone together.

'Tell me about Sofija's body, about how it feels to have sex with her,' I would sometimes ask, after love-making. 'Is it tender and soft, firm and athletic? Tell me again about her breasts, her hips, about how she moves.'

I wanted to know, to feel her, to imagine her with him, his eyes on her body. When he spoke of her, I felt her body interleaving itself between his and mine, sealing us together, rather than pulling us apart.

•

It was the summer holidays, instead, that pushed us apart for weeks on end. I went to spend time with Victor at my parents' home in Sussex. He loved the house there, the pool, my parents doting on him. Anton joined us for a while, staying briefly enough to avoid any of the usual family friction. I liked our walks in the countryside around Burgess Hill, through farmers' fields, the drives along the roads framed with manicured hedges, the soft rolling hills. We took Victor to London on day trips to see the statue of Peter Pan in Kensington Gardens and visit the Natural History Museum. Although he was keen to emphasize that he was now well out of his dinosaur phase, Victor nonetheless explained to us the differences between the diplodocus and the stegosaurus with great flourish, marching through the vaulted galleries and pointing to their most exciting specimens.

Days after Anton had gone back to Amsterdam, I left Victor in the care of my parents for a couple of days and took the train back to London where Emil came to visit. I sequestered him for one of those days in his hotel bedroom and then took him to Sir John Soane's Museum to show him another obsessive collector's environment, full of archaeological objects and plaster casts, before he left again. Around that time Anton went camping in the dunes on Vlieland with

Defne. Later, it was Anton who took Victor to his parents'
in Zeeland. I joined them for a short while. The summer
holidays were fragmented. Again, Anton and I seemed to be
doing little more than passing one another by, rarely spending more than a few days together in the same place.

As always, when I returned to Amsterdam at the end of
the summer, it was the hollyhocks that struck me at first.
They were everywhere in the city centre amidst the slender seventeenth-century gable houses, and they turned the
canal belt into illustrated pages out of a book of fairy tales.
Hollyhocks sprouted at the base of trees, grew in any small
interstices between uneven pavements, and on every patch
of dirt on the banks of canals: dark purple, pink, white and
red, they stretched to extraordinary heights, their papery
corollas gently oscillated in the breeze until they gradually
tore apart and turned into dust. The terraces of cafés now
sprawled across streets and over canal bridges; locals swam
in the IJ, and sailed small motorboats through the tree-lined
canals. Tourists clamoured on booze cruises and flocked to
the Museumplein, queuing around the block to enter the Van
Gogh Museum and the Rijksmuseum.

I was alone for a few days and cycled across the city aim-
lessly. I found myself accidentally retracing routes I had taken
before. I passed by the Portuguese café, and the many bars
where I had set up rendezvous with dozens of dates: Stefan,
Arnold, Sander and others whose names now eluded me. I
returned to concert venues and to the neighbourhoods those
encounters had taken me to, in the cold dark winter months
and the wet spring, places and routes that had once, beneath

their banal appearance, been the site of so much tension and excitement. They were now part of my secret cartography of the city. Along blocks of flats whose inhabitants had become strangers again, I could still conjure a memory of expectation, surprise and sensuousness. Now, I missed Anton, serious, reliable, supportive, a life partner who would be back in a few days' time. I missed Emil and his playfulness. He was off hiking with his daughter in the Pyrenees, and then would be back to be with Sofija. I imagined their life together, like the one I led with Anton. Unconsciously our two couples overlapped in my thoughts.

8

The Sharing Economy

I spotted the lover of my lover straight away as I stepped
inside the Roni Horn exhibition at FOAM, the photography
gallery. I did not approach her immediately, though. Instead,
I took Anton's arm and marched straight ahead through the
first room, towards the galleries at the back. It was only much
later that I crept back to the entrance of the show where Sofija
was still speaking with people, looking radiant amidst a now
thinning stream of people.

She worked the crowd with poise, a broad smile on her
face, often bursting into short sonorous laughs. Once in a
while, she lightly pressed an interlocutor's arm to express
how amused she was. Her eyes darted brightly around the
room and she locked gaze with people who briefly stopped
by to air-kiss her, or just squeeze her hand if she was already
in a conversation with someone. If not, they would jump into
a captivating exchange with her.

At least that was how it looked from the other side of the
gallery, where I stood. The bank she worked for had spon-
sored the exhibition, Anton had whispered to me when we

had arrived, seeing the look of surprise on my face, when I saw her standing in the museum's entrance like she owned the place. Looking at her now, from a safe distance, I was in awe of her ability to engage so easily in discussions with so many people. I watched as she stood, straight-backed, one hip slightly jutting forward, as her left hand rested assertively on the other hip. Her posture showed off the slim black tuxedo trousers and the oversized sleeveless organza blouse, fastened at the neck with an ample pussy bow. The shirt's translucent dusty pink fabric emphasized the tawny beige of her arms. Her flame-red lipstick poked fun at the rest of her outfit, as if to say: beware those soft, subdued colours. The contrast made her look hard and soft, opaque and translucent, approachable and inaccessible. When she laughed, she tilted her head back slightly, enough for her long side-swept fringe to reveal her forehead for an instant. I don't know how long I stayed still, absorbing each detail of her body and clothing. I had seen her before, many times, at art events, noticing every time her elegance, her confident smile and her posse of businessmen in tow. I'd had no idea who she was. I had asked around but received only the vaguest of answers. I pointed out how intimidating she seemed, but people just stared blankly.

Anton had disappeared, looking for a series of large colour photographs made in London, in which Roni Horn had repeatedly captured the Thames in close-up, revealing the changing murky tones of the water in breathtakingly subtle variations. She had also written striking, poetic texts about the river and the way it carried the city's history. Anton had fallen in love with those pictures, and with the artist's poetic voice. He had been eager to come this evening to see the show, even though the artist was not present at the opening. This evening was reserved for corporate guests, and the galleries crawled with business suits.

Everywhere outside of the gallery Amsterdam still basked in its powdery summer mode. People lingered at café terraces and cycled around the city looking relaxed. It was the last weekend before school would start again, and a few signs that things were beginning to stir appeared all across town. In different neighbourhoods, people unloaded luggage, camping and sailing gear, or unhooked bikes from contraptions fixed on overheated parked cars. Tired children drowsily stepped out onto the pavement, discombobulated by long journeys and the impending beginning of the school year.

Sofija still stood in the middle of the air-conditioned gallery space; she seemed to be its centre of gravity, hugging, shaking hands, kissing cheeks. For a while she had been speaking to an elegant elderly woman in white linen who seemed completely engrossed by what Sofija was telling her. Elbow held high, looking across the room, she pointed at two similar photographs of an owl hanging side by side. Then she flipped her hand upwards, palm open towards the sky to insist on a point she was making. She raised her shoulders in a quick shrug.

I stared at those lips Emil kissed, noting that her canines pointed slightly outwards, conveying something different than her reserved posture. She mouthed a few words and the two men in suits who had just gathered around her, and who were clearly under her spell, marched over to the bar in the gallery's lobby. She pulled out her phone and frowned at the screen. I slowly walked up to her, unsure whether she knew who I was. She looked straight through me. As I was about to retreat, I saw a flash of recognition in her eyes and she suddenly broke into a wide smile.

'Gabrielle! We finally meet! Emil has told me so much about you!'

Her voice was slightly hoarse, deep, self-assured. I tried to match her casual enthusiasm.

'Yes, finally! I have seen you around, of course, but I don't think we've ever spoken.'

'But now we are! Isn't it strange that we needed to meet the same man on a silly dating app to finally get speaking?' She opened her eyes wide as she let out one of her brief throaty laughs. I stared at the silky bangs swaying as she moved.

'I have to say . . . It took me a while to realize, after the way Emil described you, that you were who I thought you were! That unapproachable woman . . . I have admired you from afar for a long time . . . your style, I mean . . .' I blurted.

'Really?' She lifted her eyebrows in disbelief.

'You are always so put together and walking around with at least two men in grey suits.'

'Ha! That's just my job. But you know what? I also remember you, and I am happy that we are meeting at last. I remember someone telling me you were Anton's wife when I asked who that handsome woman with the unruly hair was! And, if you can believe it, I even remember seeing you once in a peacock-blue coat I coveted, and wearing a beret tilted across your head, just above your green eyes.' She raised her hand and drew an imaginary line in the air with her index finger, inches away from my forehead.

I blushed. 'Every time I see you, you are always surrounded with people, I had no idea you ever saw me.'

'Ah yes! I go to openings with clients of the bank or colleagues. But nonetheless. And believe it or not, I have even read some of your articles. You can be very persuasive when you want to make a case,' she added, with a strange smile.

Before I could answer, one of the men returned to give her a drink, and she immediately changed topics. She told me about the exhibition and her bank's sponsorship program. She had been following Roni Horn's work for years, she explained, and several works in the show were now part of the bank's collection. The man slipped away.

'You have been such a great influence on Emil,' she suddenly breathed.

'What do you mean?'

'He told me about your weekend in London together and that you dragged him to exhibitions. He said how much you encouraged him to form an opinion, to take a stand about the art you showed him.' She delved deeper into that summer trip to London that I was at pains to recognize as the sex-filled weekend I had spent with Emil. I looked down, focused on her arched feet in the pointed black slingbacks. It was strange to hear the lover of your lover share fictitious memories of time spent together. I wondered what he would make of our conversation, and said nothing.

'He also tells me he is very happy with you!' I said. 'We visit shows together mainly because, as you can tell, I am not so much of a sports buff, but I know he really likes to exercize with you.'

'Ha! Yes, but I am way more competitive than he is.' He was a complete hedonist, she went on. So many times, when they had gone on a long bike ride together, all he seemed to ever want to do was to stop in a beautiful spot, and roll around in the grass, however unsexy they both were in Lycra shorts and helmets. She laughed again. He had never mentioned anything of the sort to me.

'Maybe we should meet, the three of us, at some point, have dinner together,' she continued, cheerfully.

I said that I had seen pictures Emil took of a dinner at her house and that she seemed to be a great cook.

'Actually,' she replied, looking at me pointedly, 'I would be scared to cook for you. I tasted that orange cake you brought to Emil for his birthday. It was totally delicious. He had to take it away from me!'

What kind of game were we playing, I wondered? As we continued this slightly absurd conversation, I noticed the thin crow's feet when she laughed, I breathed in her perfume, incense-like, genderless, dry. Her eyes still occasionally checked the people passing by. A few interrupted us. She gave them a brief arm squeeze, a peck on the cheek, a dazzling smile. She would catch up with them later. She shook her head again, and I saw a small pearly white earing shining through her black hair. Moments before, I remembered glimpsing a black pearl in the other ear. They had to be intentionally mismatched, a signal to others of the host of contrasts that her entire presence exuded. I followed the line of her neck, from her ears to her broad shoulders. She worked out every day, Emil said, and being in bed with her was like being in bed with a double of himself, so similarly firm and taut were their bodies.

I stared at the woman who was intimate with my lover, unable to feel any jealousy, or embarrassment, even though I knew what her breasts were like under the organza shirt, that her hips were wider than her boyish figure suggested. I looked at her and the words used by Emil to describe her all came back. I was riveted. I snapped back to our conversation.

'It happened so fast when I met Emil. There was this incredible, self-evident chemistry. And then, it was amazing to find out we lived so close to one another.' She had a sparkle in her eyes as she spoke. It felt odd to witness her effusive feelings for a man I was also intimate with. I did not know what to say. Emil always spoke of her with such detachment, mentioning he found her a little shallow, so that I had no idea whether she was imagining things or he had not told me things as they really were. They had met at the beginning of the summer, and by then Emil had been my lover for a couple of months already. It was over those eight weeks that I had stopped seeing anyone else.

'Have you heard from him recently, since he went to the Pyrenees?'

She had not, and at that point I realized that since we had begun speaking the noise of people surrounding us in the gallery had become nothing more than a blur. The pictures on the wall had disappeared in a haze, there seemed to be nothing but us and the lingering scent of her perfume. Nothing but her body in front of me, the prominent canines that showed when she smiled, the long bangs. I thought of Emil's words when he spoke about her. Her body was there, under the tuxedo pants, under the organza shirt, her breasts, wide hips, muscular limbs. Her presence, each tremor of her body, her moving hands as she spoke, the parted lips, her dark, warm gaze superseded everything.

Suddenly, Anton appeared between us. They spoke briefly. He explained something which I did not understand but sounded vaguely like we had to be on our way. There was a moment of indecision. I excused myself and followed him out to our bikes parked on the canal. I was still in a haze by the time we arrived home to Victor and to Anton's mother who was staying with us for the last weekend of the holidays.

Later, when Victor was in bed and Anton's mother had retired for the night, I told him, hesitantly, with affected neutrality, that I had enjoyed speaking with Sofija and asked why it was that we had had to leave.

He looked at me, surprised: 'But darling, I said very clearly that I needed to go and relieve my mother but that you should feel free to stay as long as you wanted! But then you didn't answer anything and you just followed me. You looked like you had seen a ghost.'

I stayed silent, the memory of everything around Sofija dissolving as we spoke, as her hands, her hips, her smooth dark hair, came back to me. I had no recollection of that exchange with Anton. Just that impression that he was tearing me away from the place where I wanted to be. And now I wanted to go back. It was too late. When I went to bed that evening, I felt like something had been taken away from me. I was disorientated, my chest felt constricted. I wanted to cry but nothing came out. Nothing made sense.

●

Cassie was waiting for me at the usual spot in the park between the blue circular art deco tea house and a majestic oak tree. She never looked as American as in her faded hoodie and running shorts. She stopped stretching once she saw me making my way across the grass. I made a show of breaking into a jog as I came closer to her.

'Morning, sleeping beauty! What's kept you in bed so late today?' she boomed cheerfully as I approached.

'Come on, I'm only ten minutes late! You've been away for weeks!'

Cassie looked straight at me. 'I hope you are not letting that boy interfere with our running schedule! Were you with him? You seem to be seeing an awful lot of him at the moment.'

A cluster of loudly chittering parakeets flew out of the oak tree, their absinthe-green pointed tails disappearing behind the tea house.

'Oh Cassie, give me a break. Emil's on a hiking trip with his daughter. Let's run. We'll talk on the way.'

We started an easy jog, running side by side on a sandy path off the main asphalt lane in the park. Cargo bikes streamed alongside us, now emptied of their load of children, and regular bikes glided by, all at the more relaxed pace that followed the adrenaline-loaded morning rush hour.

'So finally, I met the woman Emil is seeing. This Sofija he told me so much about. She was nice, friendly. Do you know anything more about her?'

Cassie pursed her lips, eyes on the path ahead of us. 'We've only had professional dealings at the gallery. She is ultra-professional, very slick. I know she is from Bulgaria and her parents were diplomats or something like that. She must have grown up in those rather posh international circles in the Hague. Beneath the sparkly varnish I actually found her a bit dull.'

'Really?' I pulled out my phone and set the timer app. 'Let's do our first sprint: 3 ... 2 ... 1 ... Go!'

We broke into a run, alarming dog walkers accustomed to the smooth regular muted raps of joggers' feet against the tarmac, and stopped, just as suddenly, forty seconds later. I struggled to catch my breath.

'I think I'm going to die.' Panting, I asked: 'So, what does she do, exactly, Sofija?'

Looking relaxed and barely flustered from the sprint, Cassie pulled one foot up to her buttocks with her hand to stretch her thigh, and then the other, as I struggled to regain my breath. We started walking in the undergrowth, then across a black wrought-iron bridge that passed over one of the narrow areas of the lake that wound its way across the park.

'You know how corporate art collections are really big here. Every bank has one. After ING, Rabobank and ABN AMRO this is perhaps the fourth collection in size, and it is made exclusively of art made since 1980, which is pretty interesting in itself. It's more than a public relations tool for the bank and its clients, it buys into the art world, and she's basically a glorified PR for the bank. Oh, that sounds harsh. No, let's say she is the interface between the collection and the outside world: she recommends artworks to buy, exhibitions to sponsor and so on, I think. Her job, I guess, is to have a feel for what the next thing is going to be, to sniff out market trends. She's good at it, I think. She is totally square and corporate and yet has some kind of craziness about her, she blurts out these utterly weird things sometimes. But that's all I know.'

'Doesn't sound too bad,' I replied, as we resumed running again. 'She must be a really good introduction to a certain part of the art world for Emil. That's probably also what he likes about her.'

'Yeah, I hate to bad-mouth people, but Emil worked once for the gallery on a catalogue, and I thought he was such an eager beaver. I think he's deeply insecure, socially, behind all that mansplaining and hard work ethic.'

'I have asked him to be transparent with me all the time. I told him the names of the other guys I was seeing when we met: Stefan and Väinö. And I think he is being honest with me. But I don't think he is with Sofija. Can we go a bit slower?' I started walking, out of breath. 'I think I am also beginning to hate the way in which he vies for my attention all the time, like a cat who constantly brings back dead mice to its master and expects a reward.'

Cassie laughed.

'That's the whole point of seeing several men at the same time: I minimize the risk of emotions getting the best of me ... I spread my affections across the board like others spread their bets across the betting table.'

'So, is that how it works?'

'Yes. And I am beginning to miss the cool detachment of online dating. Emil is so present, so needy, somehow. He is in touch all the time. He has become almost like a second partner. But since I've heard all those lies he fed Sofija about the trip to London, I've begun to distrust him. And yet, I also feel I cannot just walk away.

'Sometimes, you know, he feels strangely absent, like an empty shell. His energy levels go right down ... Frankly, I am getting tired of his whims. And I also miss the playing around, the speed of digital dating, the quick chats.'

I started running again, slowly. 'I like that I can just walk out of a bedroom after sex and move on, not feel accountable or concerned about anything.'

Cassie now led the way, and was outdistancing me again. I raised my voice as I trailed behind her: '... not have anyone ... bother me!'

We veered away from the main path and circled around a pond surrounded by cattails and yellow irises, and then over the white metal bridge: she was obviously intent on doing a lot more interval training today. I rushed after her, panting, catching up only when she suddenly slowed down for another bout of easy running.

'It sounds like Emil has turned into husband number two. How is Anton reacting to this?'

'"Husband number two" is pushing it. But about Anton, I am not sure.'

'Have you actually spoken to him?'

'Well, yes, no, he is a bit mysterious about it all. It's clear he doesn't like the guy at all, but after all his talking about me being quote unquote agitated, whatever that means, and hopping around from one date to the other, he can hardly complain that I am settling into a more stable ... thing, whatever this thing is.'

'Don't rock the boat too much, though, you'd better talk to him more and see how he's taking it. I am not sure Marcus would be very happy to see he was shadowed by a younger, less intelligent lover – that is, of course, if we did have an open relationship, which would not work for us anyway.'

We always came back to that. I could not really answer anything – let alone explain that Anton and I did not need to check on each other all the time, that things always balanced out in the long run, that we could just let things go, unspoken. We no longer needed to periodically revisit the rules of the open marriage, or to dissect one another's each and every desire and thoughts. Cassie broke into a short sprint again and I scrambled after her.

On the recovery run that followed I told her about the party Anton had suggested we organize, a few weeks from then.

'It's really to get into the mood for the autumn, to catch up with people before everyone becomes immersed in work, while the lightness of the holidays still lingers. It's going to be a Wednesday late afternoon and evening: drinks, things to eat, something relaxed, not too late.'

'Great, tell me what you want me to bring and if you need a hand setting up.' She asked if I would invite Sofija. I had planned to ask Emil to bring her. Would Cassie help me plan the food and guestlist?

'Sure. But first, come on, last sprint, and then we'll go and stretch in the rose garden.'

Roni Horn, Foam Fotografiemuseum
Amsterdam, 30 August 2014

I pressed ahead, letting go of Anton's arm. I knew the pictures were waiting for me there, in the gallery at the back of the museum.

One hundred photographs in colour and black and white, presented in a single row like a continuous ribbon lining the four walls of a room. *Roni Horn, You are the Weather, 1994–1995.* Each image slightly wider than A4 size, unframed, hanging at eye level, almost identical to the next, shows the face of Margrét, nothing more. I knew they had been made during a six-week trip to Iceland when the artist and Margrét had travelled to the hot springs and natural pools that dot the island. In each picture, Margrét stares at the photographer, head emerging from the water. Her skin moist, dewy, surrounded by the vapour of a warm pool. She has a sharp, hard gaze in some images, a questioning one in others, a bored, perhaps irritated look in a few of them. In several pictures, Margrét almost vanishes in a white haze. The changing Icelandic weather reflects on her face, on the light that colours the water around her: turquoise, ultramarine, greyish, whitish. Margrét, twenty-four, twenty-five years old in the pictures, would be my age now. But there she is, ageless, looking back at the woman who photographs her, who captured her image anew every day, every day in a different light. Margrét's damp hair, the moistness of her skin freshly dipped in the water, showered by the rain, her coral lips. Her face, the unique prism through which the artist looks at the world. Is that an image of love, the object of love conferring her glow to the world, becoming, for the other, an unsurpassable horizon?

Photographer and model responded to one another in the photographic act. And now, standing amidst these pictures, I feel it is my turn to uphold Margrét's gaze, that Roni Horn is asking me to become more than a witness. As I look at the many expressions on the face of Margrét I see desire, rejection, patience, impatience, boredom, excitement, togetherness, and I see the artist's invitation to others to elucidate that encounter. I walk up to one of the pictures, and stand very close, caressing it with my eyes, taking in the freckles and the tiny marks on Margrét's skin. Her inquisitive eyes stare at me from their immobile position on the wall. I decide to walk back to the entrance and introduce myself to Sofija.

9

You Are The Weather

'Sure, let's meet for lunch! The next two weeks, my diary is a horror, but what about Sunday thirteenth?'

It had taken Cassie the entire weekend to find me Sofija's mobile number, purportedly to invite her to the party. It was my ingenious alternative plan to get hold of it without Emil being involved. I had asked him for it first, casually, and when he had breezily answered back 'Sure', I knew he would make sure he never sent it. And then I had spent hours thinking up a number of excuses I could use to ring her until I decided that I needed none. I just wanted to see her again, to continue our conversation, to bask in her aura again for a little while. The chat we had had at the exhibition opening made it plain to me that our meeting was long overdue.

It took Sofija another twenty-four hours to get back to me. I had proposed a drink, she suggested lunch. When I hung up the phone on her enthusiastic voice, I pondered her choice of words: 'my diary is a horror' – who would speak like that? I wondered if it might be a Dutch phrase, lost in translation. Still. I had my rendezvous, two weeks from now, but possibly earlier. When she had announced her next availability two weeks away, my heart had sunk. I had asked if, like my hair-dresser, she might consider putting me on a waiting list in case she had a gap in her diary before then. She hadn't missed a beat; had agreed and then teasingly offered to give me a haircut as well – that would be, she assured me, edgier than the one I usually got at my usual place. Her remark had shut me up for a few days. I was happy she had responded to my quip with a joke and then slightly put off by her rudeness.

Emil, chirpily and unknowing, texted me a few days later, to say that Sofija had just left his studio after dropping by for a coffee, and confided her impressions of our encounter at the Roni Horn exhibition. Cycling home, he reported, she said she could only think of what it would be like to see me and him making love. She said she thought of the curves of my body under my summer dress, the curves he had described to her. She had reiterated the wish for a dinner bringing the three of us together. I answered that I was surprised, flattered, amused, and moved on to another topic while I thought back about her slightly crooked teeth, her dazzling smile and the bra strap showing under the organza shirt.

Cassie had also found out where she lived, a quiet back street behind the Albert Cuyp market in the Pijp area, over-looking the Sarphatipark, and so I had proposed to meet in her neighbourhood, at the Ijsbreker. It was one of the very few places in Amsterdam that reminded me of a Parisian brasserie, a nineteenth-century café overlooking the Amstel river. On the agreed Sunday, I parked my bike on the other side of the river, by the park, amidst the crisp dry leaves of the plane trees that had fallen abruptly, in the abnormally dry days of the end of the summer.

The terrace was sprawling on each side of the Weesperzijde, the street that ran along the river. Waiters and waitresses attired in long white aprons navigated perilously amidst the bikes, as they crossed the street walking from the restaurant to the terrace on the riverbank. I looked at their skilful ballet between the bicycles as I waited for her, at a table under the trees, next to the water.

She arrived late, glowing, in white palazzo pants and a black sleeveless top, and stood for a while beside the table, a hand on her hip, in that old-fashioned pose I had seen her take at the museum, making a show of inhaling the dry papery smell of the elms alongside the water.

'Sunday! How wonderful!' she exhaled as she fell in the rattan armchair chair next to me, a slight squeeze on my shoulder.

'I went out for a bike ride early this morning and I am ravenous!' I did not dare ask with whom.

'I just mentioned to him we were meeting,' she said, as if reading my thoughts. 'He didn't seem to know,' she added, casually.

It was strange to be in her presence again after these two weeks, after these years of seeing her from a distance, after all of Emil's words about her. She exuded life and spoke directly, with no ambiguity. She said she lived very close by, on the other side of the river.

'This is a classic Amsterdam place, I love it. I often come in the morning, after a run, to have a coffee and look at

the riverbanks lined with houseboats.' She mentioned the
particular quality of the morning light over the Amstel. A
waiter came by carrying a couple of menus. She accepted
one with a smile and appeared to lose herself in its
contemplation.

'Do you know who Renée Perle was?' I blurted out the
name, without thinking. I had just realized. The hand on
the hip, the other day at the museum, and just now, in the
summer light. The palazzo pants, the tank top. She was
an almost perfect reincarnation of the Romanian model
Jacques-Henri Lartigue had photographed in the 1930s on
the Côte d'Azur.

'Renée who?'

'Perle, with an e. A model, from the thirties.'

I told her about those images that had fascinated me as a
teenager and had given Lartigue some of his best shots. Renée
at the beach, looking away, casually lounging, images that
were incredibly modern, that could have been made yester-
day. I did a quick internet search and showed her pictures of
a tall slender woman in her twenties, with dreamy eyes and a
heart-shaped mouth, dressed very much like Sofija was today.
Beautiful, slightly aloof.

The waiter came by and took our orders. There were no
houseboats moored along the part of the riverbank next to
where we sat, under a double row of elms. We looked at the
small motorboats steering along the river.

'I think I know of Lartigue,' Sofija said. 'Wasn't he that
upper-class Parisian boy who was given a camera by his
parents and became one of the very first photographers to

capture movement, as in old race cars and so on, at the beginning of the twentieth century?'

I acquiesced. She continued, 'I don't know much of his later work. What happened to Renée Perle after Lartigue stopped taking photos of her?'

'I am not sure. She lived in the South of France. I think she became a painter.' I had researched her some years back and come across a picture of her standing amidst self-portraits that all seemed to be based on the photographs made by Lartigue. It had been strange to discover that the image she had of herself seemed to be the one created by her photographer lover. It was as if the pictures of Lartigue both affirmed her existence and made her disappear behind the image that he had left behind for posterity.

Sofija looked at me thoughtfully and mused:

'Do you realize that years ago that question about what happened to Renée Perle, or who she was, would not even have crossed our minds? Like for years, André Breton's Nadja, the woman he took as model for his best book and then abandoned in an asylum. I mean, that is the gist of it. So, like Nadja, Renée Perle was a muse, one of those women whom people know little about because nobody cared, beyond the great works they inspire. What happened to all those muses who died destitute?'

She let her question hang in the air.

'But now we are beginning to revise all those histories, to look at them, to question the idea of the muse. Feminism has done some work there, thankfully.'

'Are you thinking of Roni Horn's photographs of Margrét? She is more than a muse, don't you think?'

'She is. But that's because her full name is credited. But it is also because of her attitude in the pictures, the way she holds the gaze of Roni Horn: these things tell us she is not a passive sitter. In fact, she shows us how photography at its best is a dialogue between sitter and photographer. It is great that your bank supports her work.'

The dishes arrived, in gleaming white porcelain: raw fish with small glasses of vodka to accompany it, rucola surrounding a soft round mound of cream-filled burrata dotted with cherry tomatoes, shiny roasted beets with crumbly goat cheese, and caramelized Swiss chard. The waiters dexterously manoeuvred across the street separating the restaurant from the terrace, balancing large trays, as the bikes slid alongside them, only occasionally stopping to let them walk over the street, most often veering from their lane to avoid them.

I asked her about the bank, told her how far that world seemed to me, asked why it was sponsoring shows and building art collections. She gave me a professional, efficient look:

'It's simple. Fine art has always been a global asset class, and it is even more so today despite the financial crisis of 2008, when Lehman Brothers went bust, and the Lehman art collection was sold. The bank builds a collection to show a way forward to its clients, to tell them that they should consider investing in art and to reassure them about it. But also, we do it to show the art world that we treat art seriously, respectfully. And then, we also create a context for bringing these worlds together, to make it clear to our clients that art is not only a valuable and diversified asset class, but that it is also a social context that is attractive to them as a status symbol.'

I shrugged. 'Isn't that completely fake? Doesn't it instrumentalize art and turn it into lifestyle?'

'I don't think so. I am passionate about art, I just want to share that passion with many people, and this is the way I do it best.'

She lifted her large sunglasses to give me a smile. There was such a distance between that kind of talk and the art world I knew. Academia, art education, art criticism, the world of artists who carefully ignored or wanted to ignore the art market.

The vodka contributed to bridge those discrepancies between what I had determinedly called her world and my world. We shared the platters of food, catching small bites from one plate and the other, commenting on how the flavours of each mixed best.

She told me anecdotes about her art world, and I about mine. We left stories unfinished because we had more stories to tell. We covered the past decade of the art world in Amsterdam through opposed perspectives. We filled in each other's fragmentary knowledge.

We moved on to the subject of online dating. She was largely a monogamist, she said, but mostly a workaholic. The conversation moved to Emil and I asked how their affair was going, how they had met, how it felt.

'It seems to be so fluid and easy between us, like we have known each other all along. We are taking things slowly, but I like the way it is going. He says the affair you had a few months back really helped him to focus more, to find some gravitas in things.'

I cleared my throat. 'What did Emil tell you about us?'

'That you met online, that you are married and have a child, that you challenge him intellectually – which is good! That you saw tons of exhibitions together,' she paused, looking for the right words, 'that sexually, you enjoy things like no one else he ever met, that you were ravenous, had orgasms by the dozen!' She laughed.

'Is that really true?' She lifted her sunglasses again and threw me a teasing glance.

'He said that you were joyful, sensuous, that he could confide in you, that you were not judgemental. And then he said that he needed a proper relationship, a monogamous one, and that you had stopped seeing each other.'

I did not tell her just then that it was far from over between Emil and me, at least as far as I knew, but this new lie, after the ones she had inadvertently revealed at the photography museum, irked me.

She was beaming. 'It feels very special to have met you, after knowing all these things.'

'I am glad our affair has left him with good memories,' I murmured, watching as she combed her slick black hair through her fingers, lost in her thoughts.

'He told me you separated because he felt it was too unbalanced, with your husband, and that he is ready for something ... real.'

'Real' hung in the air. She was intoxicating. Lively, very real, sitting beside me.

I stood up.

'Let's make a move, get coffee somewhere else. Walk a bit, shall we?' She looked up at me, eyes questioning, and slowly rose from the table.

We agreed to go Dutch, chased the waiter and settled the bill. We walked side by side in silence under the trees, to the bridge. I suggested a walk in the Sarphatipark. She took my arm with a new familiarity as we crossed the bridge. I wondered if she knew what a pack of lies Emil had fed her, that only two days ago I had gone by his studio for a brief tryst before he was set to meet her, that he spoke of her casually as an affair amidst others. I wondered if she could sense it, that the story she told me was mostly just a tale.

We wandered into the park.

'The Scandinavian Embassy over there on the other side of the park is supposed to have the best coffee in town, isn't it?'

She smiled: 'That's where I buy stocks of it to keep at home.'

We walked around the pond, across the lawn where children played football and up to the monument to Samuel Sarphati. The bust under the heavily ornamented canopy had been removed by the Nazis when they occupied Amsterdam, she told me.

'They renamed the park after the founder of Dutch fascism, Gerard Bolland, did you know that?' I replied. 'Sarphati's bust was returned to the park immediately after the war. Amazing how much the Nazis cared for details such as changing park names, in the middle of the war. As if deporting Jews was not enough.'

The Netherlands was where the greatest percentage of

Jewish population out of all of Western Europe was mur-
dered. That had been one of the first things I had learnt when
I had come to Amsterdam. The myth of Anne Frank had been
bust within weeks of my moving to the Netherlands.

'Yes, indeed,' she said. 'And I think the changing of the
park's name was part of that vision the Nazis had, that an ideological revolution was possible here, because of the cultural
proximity between Germany and the Netherlands. The kind
of thing that begins unconsciously with small gestures, like
removing busts and changing the names of parks.'

We fell silent and looked at the kids playing, the adults
walking in twos, pushing prams or sat on benches chatting
and enjoying the last bits of summer, the sun that sprayed
through the branches of the trees and lapped the surface of
the water and the lawns.

I liked to feel her body moving next to mine, taller, slimmer, stronger, as we walked. I could sense its outline under
the thin clothing as she ambled across the grass.

'Have you ever slept with women, or had affairs with
women?' she suddenly asked.

I replied I had always been attracted to women but not had
any affairs since my twenties.

'I never managed to somehow find an entrance into that
world'. I had visited most of the lesbian bars in Amsterdam,
from the historic Café Saarein in the Jordaan, to the hipper
Vivelavie, near the Rembrandtplein, but each time, had felt
like I was an intruder. 'And then the few times in my life I
have tried to flirt with a woman I have been made painfully
aware that I was barking up the wrong tree.'

Sofija emitted a soft laugh and told me some stories of hers. They were mysterious, unclear, unfinished. A dinner party somewhere where she had followed a woman going to the restrooms, and found herself leaving the restaurant with her and not coming back. Another time, sharing a taxi in New York. Not always believable, they added nonetheless to the elusiveness she projected, the woman and her posse of businessmen in suit, as I still pictured her.

'This is where I live.' She pointed at a late nineteenth-century façade made of smooth ochre bricks and wrought-iron balconies, just outside the park.

'Number 63, with the balcony there, supported by the stone lion heads. Come. I will make you that coffee from the Scandinavian Embassy. I might also have a little dessert for us.'

She showed me around her small apartment. Tidy, precise, a flat for one with carefully chosen photographs and paintings displayed on the walls. She left me on the balcony while she went to make coffee, and I observed the clutches of people below who wandered in and out of the park and queued up at the ice-cream van at the corner of the street. The ornate black-metal enclosure, the nineteenth-century English garden reminded me of London squares, save for the narrower and lower buildings that enclosed it.

I went back inside, and circled around her, looking distractedly at the objects, the books on the coffee table, the papers on her desk. She had kicked off her espadrilles when she had walked into the flat and trod on the floorboards and the thick rug in her bare feet, each toe sending out little sparks of bright red as she motioned around, picked up cups, coffee, glasses of water.

I wanted to kiss her.

'Coffee. Hold on, I also have some raspberries, they are very sweet!'

I looked at her; I felt like an idiot – when, abruptly, she seized one of the small juicy pink, hollow fruits between her fingers and placed it in my mouth; the sweet-sour fragrant fruit crushed between my teeth.

'May I kiss you?' I whispered

She smiled. I approached my lips to hers. We kissed, and the softness of her skin struck me. It was so different from that of a man. Soft, moist, infinitely desirable. We pulled away, staring at each other. Surprise or triumph, I could not really say. We kissed again. Desire surged, receded and surged again. She was a stranger, perhaps she could become a friend, she was an object of my desire. Each thought came in as a wave, was cancelled by the next, and then returned following the ebb and flow of my desire.

We kissed standing in the middle of her living room and I suddenly felt her hand tugging at the belt of my dress, untying it. I reached out and felt her firm thigh under the thin fabric of her pants. I nudged away her bra, under the black top, pushed it up to reveal a small, pointed breast. I stopped and looked. There was nothing more erotic, more exquisite, more exciting than this small breast popping out from under the black cloth. I traced its outline with my finger, its perfect outline: the breast of Lee Miller in pictures by Man Ray. I let my fingers follow the areola, I brushed past her hardened nipple. I pulled up the rest of her top. And looked at her.

She casually pulled me towards her and somehow comically frog-marched me backwards to her bedroom without saying a word. She pulled off my dress, and looked for a moment at my coordinated dark green underwear, joking that hers looked way shabbier but extremely comfortable. Her dexterity surprised me: my bra snapped open in a second. She pressed her body against mine. Her small firm breasts against my larger heavy ones. The sensation was dizzying. The softness of her skin, of a woman's skin, gave me the impression that our two bodies were merging into one. The curves of her body were soft, incredibly desirable. I remembered what Emil had told me, her small heavy breasts, her tightness, her difficulty to reach orgasm. But now I also began to see everything Emil had not told me about. I saw the tight texture of her skin, the dark silky tuft of hair between her thighs, the muscular legs. I felt her small hand touching me, caressing my face. The lightness of her body struck me after years, and especially months, of sex with men. I felt a closeness, a familiarity: I knew what a woman's body was like, I knew what I could do with it, I wanted her to squirm and shout; I wanted to look at her while she shivered and squirmed around on her bed. She pinned me down, laughed, gently bit my nipples. I felt matronly against her agility, against her lean strong limbs.

I took over and kissed her, caressed the golden vellus hair that ran across her lower belly and felt the smoothness of her skin in the inside of her thighs. She shivered as my fingers and then my tongue crept up the inside of her thighs toward the black glistening tuft of hair. I wanted her to come under my fingers, to hear her gasp, and feel the contractions of her vagina.

She escaped from my arms and pushed me down on the bed and I remembered that there is no straightforward narrative arc in sex between women. There are many side stories, many beginnings and many ends. She slithered alongside my body, recoiling as I tried to grasp her, dancing around me in the bed. She pressed me down and rubbed my clit, pushed her slender fingers into me. She enjoyed seeing me at her mercy, as she slid over and under my body. 'Come,' she ordered.

Pleasure came in waves. Later, she retreated and let me touch her, lick, seize her hard nipples and squeeze them as she had done with the raspberry earlier on, and then she came forward again and caressed my body striated with stretchmarks, soft and ample. She was all tension and muscle, from her back to her spherical buttocks which felt cool under my hand. I saw her even, tawny skin contrast with my pronounced suntan lines, pink toes and white belly. She withdrew from my embraces unpredictably and then returned, like a dragonfly circling around, prodding me and slipping away each time that I felt I was gaining the upper hand. Finally came the moment.

'I am coming!' she whispered, letting go of my hair.

Later, we lay together listening to the sounds coming from the park as the colour of the sky changed to the pinkish-orange hue of late afternoon. She was on her belly, resting on her forearms, knees bent, swinging her feet crossed at the

ankles. She stretched her neck and lo
beyond the bed, to the main room and
French windows. The dampness of the par
day permeated the air, carrying indoors the
trodden grass and dust. We listened to the dim
of children playing in the park, a few deeper voice   parents
herding the little ones for bath time, dinner time.

Then came the lively evening symposium of starlings. We
listened to the murmuration as it fluttered from canopy to
canopy, and then chirruped, tweeted and sang as the pink
sky turned a deeper blue.

The faint bell of the trams signalled a life beyond the park,
the hum of the city in motion, while I lay beneath her, on my
back, motionless in the shadow of the bed. Her breasts pro-
truded from her raised torso, two small pointed cones with
indecently shaped nipples inches away from my face. Once
again, I let my finger trace the line of her neck, follow the
curve of her shoulder and glide to her breast.

'Did you always know you that you liked women?' I
asked. 'I mean, do you define yourself as queer, or bisexual?'
I observed the slight movement of the wrinkled brown flesh
of her large nipples above me, the sphinx-like expression of
her face, features still drawn towards the window.

'Oh, I am not bisexual.'

The conclusive note in the voice.

She slipped out of the bed, stood there against the light, in
the middle of the room. The outline of her body was a cut-out
against the darkening sky and the blackened leaves of the
park trees. Without a word she went and wrapped herself in

ght cotton robe and walked through to the living room where she closed the French windows. The glorious symphony of twittering birds abruptly ceased.

●

David was waiting for me seated at the bar on the ground floor of the Stedelijk museum. It was a quiet spot for Monday morning coffee. We were alone, aside from a few random tourists and tall Dutch businessmen in flashy suits and brown pointy shoes. From where he sat, David could survey the entrance to the Design Museum on the other side of the green. I wondered briefly if that was why he came here almost every morning.

'Gabrielle! Thank you for being free on a Monday morning like this. I wanted to meet you here because there is this terrific film piece upstairs in the museum, *Dissonant*, by this Dutch artist, Manon de Boer. Do you know her? She lives in Brussels. Her work is rarely shown here.'

'I've heard about it, not seen it yet.'

'It's brilliant. It's about dance and music and the tangibility of all those things.' He gestured animatedly. 'Let's go upstairs and watch it together after our little chat.' He sighed, 'I need more art in my life! The team is doing great work, their plans are fantastic. But I miss something sensitive, tactile, like the breathing sound of the dancer in this film. You will see. So, tell me, how are you getting on with your proposal?'

'I have something for you, but maybe you can first tell me more about the direction the Design Museum is going in?'

'Of course. So, we have approached quite a few people

and the subject is striking a chord. Smartphones and social networks have now been around for long enough that people feel they are able to think along with us and participate in the project. People realize that this digital economy is changing their life in a profound way, and they want to react to this phenomenon. The whole field we are investigating is so plagued with paradoxes and dichotomies and the views of the team are too polarized, too much oriented towards defining positives and negatives. I think we need more nuance.'

David took a sip of his coffee.

'For instance, you can argue that social media tends to lock individuals up inside themselves, right? Or you can argue the exact opposite, that it facilitates contacts between people. Both statements are valid, so the question really is about the nature of digital interactions: are they standardized because they are filtered by algorithms and by our self-branding on social media? Perhaps it's more accurate to say that we "connect" with one another,' David mimed inverted commas and emphasized each syllable of the key words, 'rather than "encounter" others, which implies more of a dynamic exchange between people. And there's another thing: we are constantly faced with our own image when we reach out to others, make profile pics and do video calls. We see ourselves all the time and we must also keep up with that image of ourselves.'

David toyed with his coffee cup, looked outside, pensively, towards the Design Museum and then back at me.

'That point connects to the opposition between what is freeing and what binds us. Digital technology both enables us to do things differently ... more efficiently, or at least it gives us that idea. It opens up possibilities and at the same time, it turns us into slaves; it both frees up time and makes us waste more time than ever and become prisoner of our own image. These things are all part of the same movement. The sharing economy is a well-chosen name. It purports to obliterate possessiveness: you invite a stranger to occupy your bed, you share collections of videos and books stored on a server, but in the end, that sharing is mostly an illusion, it is more like permanent rental. In that sense, this type of sharing belongs to a traditional system of capitalist exchange.'

'And,' I added, trying to follow his train of thoughts, 'I think we experience things at a faster rate too, don't you think? We sample homes, music, people and then move on. It undoubtedly changes our experience of the world.'

'Interesting,' murmured David. 'I have been thinking the exhibition perhaps could have different paces ... something like fast and slow sections. Sections that absorb the viewer's attention, and others that keep visitors at a distance, just like that piece upstairs, *Dissonant*.'

'Actually, that sounds a little like what I have come to imagine for the exhibition. When you first asked me to curate it, I imagined you wanted me to show artwork about robotics, that kind of thing. But in the past months, I felt the need to slow down, I've wanted to explore how experience is embodied, how it goes through technology but also through the body.'

I opened the notebook resting on the table and glanced briefly at my notes:

'So, my starting point was to think about the way that computers, video games, smartphones and so on, all these digital tools tend to make us forget about our bodies. We sink into a sofa in a really awkward position without noticing it until we get completely stiff, we get RSI from hours at the computer, that kind of thing. But that's just one small way in which our body is involved. I have found myself looking at a wall map on the metro almost trying to zoom in with two fingers as if enlarging a photograph on my phone. We spend so much time exploring the world through digital tools that we momentarily forget about the space we occupy in real life, the speed we walk at, and so on.'

'Absolutely. You see people bumping into one another so much more nowadays than pre-smartphone.' David sighed.

I nodded. 'So, with that in mind, I thought it would be great to incite people to reappropriate their body, to think about the way they look, breathe, occupy space, about the complexity, the richness of embodiment.'

I pulled out a folded sheet of paper with a list of names and works printed on it.

'And what better for that than to show analogue films, dance pieces and photographs, all works that engage in a dialogue between technology and the body?'

I listed the works. The films and dance pieces, the photography series that had been floating in my mind for all these months, works that showed me directions when I was lost, or simply that calmed me. There was Anne Teresa de Keersmaeker's solo piece, danced to the music of Joan Baez, and there was Roni Horn's photo series, *You are the Weather*.

Next on the list was Lucinda Childs, and I explained how the video recording of the same ballet superimposed itself on the ballet performed live in the theatre, and then also, there was *Facing Forward*, the found footage film by Fiona Tan.

'I think I still need a fifth piece. I noticed, when I began to think of these works together, that all of them engage with technology that is almost obsolete: analogue photograph, LP record player, early video, and the hand-wound camera. Because they all feature the human body, these works have an immediate presence but they also take you to another place and time through the obsolete technology they display. It is this dynamic movement between something that is mediated and the immediacy of the present moment that I find so interesting. It is within this dynamic movement that encounters can take place. These works of art make us see the world in a different way; they reveal a world that we remember once existed; they activate a vision of the past. And they help us to imagine the future.'

David nodded slowly.

'I like it,' he said, pensively. 'I think I get it and I think we could pull it off. And I like showing these artworks and dance pieces that have been seen across town this year, pieces that many people will have seen. It adds something about the information loop, about seeing and seeing again, and it is also about the institution as a medium, a little like a computer or a phone screen'.

We talked more about how it could work in the space of the Design Museum and then David stood up.

'Let's go up and look at this film piece I mentioned earlier. Maybe that could be your fifth work for the show.'

I followed David into the small, carpeted dark room at the top of the monumental staircase of the Stedelijk museum. Several people were walking out.

'Good,' said David, 'I think we are arriving just before it begins.' Inside, one of the benches was occupied by a couple of women quietly chatting in the semi-darkness. We waited for the performance to begin.

Manon de Boer, Stedelijk Museum Amsterdam, 14 September 2014

The screen remains dark as the sparkling first notes of a musical score played on a violin begin to fill the small dark room of the museum. Within seconds, the music becomes more dramatic and solemn. A clicking sound and the screen lights up to reveal a woman in an empty room, facing the camera. Behind her, floor-to-ceiling windows look out onto a canopy of leafy trees.

The woman stands still as the music begins to alternate between high-pitched staccato and more austere passages. She seems to follow its rhythm attentively, nodding slightly, pursing her lips, murmuring the tune. She breathes deeply as she takes in its brusque passages and occasional dissonances.

The music stops. The woman takes a step back from the camera, tilts her head up and moves into a backward swing. She follows it with a tilt to the side that now sets her entire body into motion. She turns away from the camera, shuffles backwards and begins to execute a choreography full of abrupt and disconnected gestures. She jigs backwards, collapses to the floor, springs up again immediately. Her breathing becomes heavier. It is, along with the shuffle of her bare feet across the floorboards, the only sound that accompanies her dancing.

The camera pans the room, following her and keeping her in the middle of the frame as it captures every one of her moves. And then suddenly the screen turns to black with a faint repeated clicking sound. Although there is no image, the sounds of her breathing and dancing continue as before. A minute or so earlier when we saw her dancing across the room, a mask of concentration on her face, we could match her movements with the memory of the music that we heard at the beginning of the film. Now, as we sit, staring at a blank screen, we must imagine the music and her movements through the breathing, the thudding, the shuffling: those fragile but pregnant signs of a human body in motion.

The sound of the switch again, and then the dancing woman reappears. Jerky motions alternate with harmonious passages that amplify the variations of the music, at least the echo of it that remains in our heads. A tiny movement of the wrist, a rotation, reaching her elbow, the rest of her arm, her shoulder and then her entire body which suddenly begins to twirl like a falling leaf.

And then she rises again, tilts her head back as if she were falling backwards and pulls herself out of the frame of the image, a gesture that is now somewhat familiar so that when the roll of film ends abruptly again, I can just about imagine what she does next. A few more minutes and then sound disappears and the credits roll.

The spectators around us stir and walk out while David

sits in silence beside me until the film, playing on a loop, resumes. The blank screen, the dazzling introductory notes, the solemn passages, the staccato rhythm, the dissonances, the long-drawn-out notes. And then the dancer listening to the music, the music that stops as the woman begins to dance, the jerky movements, the rotation of the wrist, the twirl like a falling leaf. I now see how she runs, walks, shuffles and skips until her energy is depleted, until she collapses and rises again. The image disappears. Her breathing fills the room, the sounds of her body on the studio floor.

David, his roundish face tense as he looks at the screen, is riveted, hands on his knees, on the rudimentary museum bench. The film tells a story broken into many pieces, forcing us to find the harmony in its disjointed parts, but telling us also that life continues even when it is unreported.

I thought of Emil's continuous messaging, his recounting of everything he did, so that sometimes I imagined that nothing happened to him if he did not tell me about it. And I thought of those men on the dating app. Of conversations that might be resumed weeks after they had begun as if time had not gone by, as if lives had been frozen while they were out of sight. But the film shows that life, like dance, goes on even if it is not filmed, photographed, or otherwise recorded.

'The film is only ten minutes long, I think,' David whispered. 'But each time I come back and sit here in the gallery, I watch it at least three times in a row.'

10

Reboot

I was halfway up the stairs when the doorbell rang.

'I'll get it,' shouted Anton.

'Thanks. Still need to change, won't be a minute!' I quickened my pace up the stairs to the landing and leapt into the bedroom. Seconds later, I recognized the drawn-out inflections of Ruedi and Anneli, Anton's impeccably punctual Swiss colleagues.

I began to rummage through my closet for something to wear. Nothing too fancy. Anything clean would do, at this point. I sighed. This morning, as the last spinach spanakopita was about to go into the oven, Anton had waltzed into the kitchen wearing an elegant baby-blue suit unseen since our wedding.

'Ha! What do you think? It still fits!' He had explained with a wide smile how he had rediscovered it at the back of his closet and how it had made him think that since the party was on the same day of the month as our wedding day, we should also celebrate our anniversary. It was, after all, six years and four months, 'to the day'. The suit still fitted him perfectly. He'd picked it up, off the rack, at Dries van Noten's so-called 'Modepaleis' as his Antwerp store was known. We had taken the train there especially as soon as we had settled the wedding date and decided to splash out on clothes from the summer collection to wear as wedding outfits. We had spent hours under the bemused eyes of the shop assistants, running up and down the store's wood-panelled grand staircase from the men to the women's department and back again, pulling out suits and dresses from the racks and laying them side by side to find the perfect match. In the end we had found the slim-fitting light blue suit, made in an oddly shimmering seersucker fabric, and paired it with a teal-coloured shirt that had now disappeared, as had my dress, a silk knee-length shift with a boat neck and short sleeves, dyed in a dazzling gradation of colours from burnt ochre to pale lemon. Anton had seemed disappointed when I reminded him that I had worn the dress all summer and every summer since then, and that in the end it had faded and frayed under the arms and was now in permanent residence in a box somewhere in the attic.

There was nothing as sunny and joyful in my wardrobe these days. After a little hesitation I picked a sleeveless, loose grey dress, with a matching belt, and dug out the invisible knickers the garment's thin fabric required. It was a pair of shapeless-looking knickers, but 'super comfortable', as Sofija would say – as she had effectively said a few days before, pointing at her own similarly drab underwear as I undressed her. I heard Anton call from below.

'I'm coming,' I shouted back, as I clipped my bra and pulled the silky grey fabric over my head. 'I am coming': those had been her exact words a few days earlier, when she had come in my arms. A good example of a performative speech act if ever there was one. I smiled. This need she had had to utter those words at exactly the moment: was it to reassure me? To make explicit something she thought I might otherwise not pick up on? I thought about her signalling this to the men she slept with. To men in need of reassurance, never sure they were 'doing it right', men who perhaps craved to hear those words to feel empowered.

If I had to admit it, making her come had given me a sense of power I rarely felt with men, the belief that I had mastered a skill, that I had prevailed with this woman who, days before, had reduced me to silence simply by the way she stood in a room. Did men ever feel that way? I remembered Heiko's proud smiles when I tried to explain the intensity of pleasure I felt with him. For a brief moment, Sofija's words had made me feel in control, and that she was grateful. And yet, just as suddenly, the situation had flipped and I had realized how naïve that thought was. She had turned me into a passive object of her desire, driving me into accepting caresses and nudges, whatever form they took, and my body had responded, accepted and enjoyed every bit of it. And now, her painted toenails, the quality of her skin, the roundness of her buttocks, the warmth between her legs had become a known territory. One that Emil had described to me many times, I now knew at first-hand.

I had not heard from her since departing from her flat on

Sunday, and had heard nothing from him for even longer. I hoped that she would come tonight. The doorbell rang again. I tied the belt loosely around my waist, and applied a dab of mascara, a smear of dark lipstick and massaged a little blush on my cheeks.

Downstairs, Anton was outside on the balcony chatting with the Swiss artist duo who had come for a year to Amsterdam as visiting professors at the academy and a younger couple I had never met before. I checked the piles of plates and rows of glasses on the table, made sure that every dish had its serving spoon. I was happy to leave the entertaining part to Anton as long as I could cook my heart out.

Cooking for numbers was the only way to do it, the only real form of cooking. It took me back to the large family gatherings of my childhood, and to the long-drawn-out process that resulted in tables covered in arrays of dishes of assorted colours, textures and flavours. The Ashkenazi and Sephardi sides of the family each had their own secrets and recipes. I often made my own, but adopted their habit of cooking for a whole day or two to host parties, preparing simultaneously stuffed vegetables and pies, salads of cooked vegetables seasoned with elaborate spice mixes, and cakes. Like my aunts, I roasted aubergines directly on the gas ring, but unlike them, when I removed the charred skin, I beat the pulp with tahini and lemon juice and not olive oil as they had taught me. Against the scepticism of the Sephardi side and the incomprehension of my Ashkenazi aunt, I made large Greek-style spinach and cheese pies, spanakopita, for which I hunted down packs of filo dough in the Turkish supermarkets in the Pijp neighbourhood. And then I prepared dozens of little lamb turnovers that required conscientious pinching and prodding to seal the dough and I baked them, which was anathema to my aunts who swore by deep-frying only.

I knew that these culinary marathons were mostly incomprehensible to many of Anton's Dutch friends, who for a party, would order catering, book a location or only serve snacks. I justified it by putting forward my Jewishness and my inherited family traditions. I pointed to the books by Claudia Roden and Ottolenghi and Tamimi's *Jerusalem* on the shelves in the kitchen and told them how my aunts would deride them when I dared read out a recipe over the phone. Each time I called one of my aunts, they inevitably ended up ordering me to take a pen and paper and listen carefully to the 'correct' recipe for the brick with tuna and potato, the challah bread and the boulous. They had always been prepared in this particular way in the family, using idiosyncratic measurement units that included the half-eggshell, the small glassful and the generous pinch. People laughed when I told them the stories but food was always a way to mask my uneasiness in those circles, to reach out to people and communicate in ways other than with words.

The doorbell was now ringing at regular intervals, preceding the ascent of individuals to the flat, couples and trios who then moved through into the living room and the open kitchen where Marcus had set up a Moscow Mule production line, turning out cocktails speedily as the number of guests grew. They were for the most part friends of Anton's and artists and colleagues from the art academy, acquaintances from art institutions, friends randomly encountered in our years in Amsterdam. Next to those there were old friends from his primary school years that Anton, like many Dutch people I knew, still met up with regularly. Anton moved confidently from one set of people to the next, making introductions and pointing out connections and shared interests between individuals. From the corner of my eye, I saw him showing off his suit to someone I did not know and telling them its story.

Victor buzzed in and out of the living room. He had lent a hand with the cooking but I wasn't sure he really enjoyed our parties, the temporary disruption of his habits and invasion of his personal space, but he liked to stick around for a while, absorbing the words and the movements of the adults around him.

I walked around, checking the buffet and joining groups of people. I sampled moods and conversations, unable to focus for more than a few minutes, and then moved on. It was good to see people in high spirits and enjoying themselves, enthusiastic about the year ahead. Parties at home had always reassured me. They mapped out the different constellations of friends and acquaintances amidst which we had built our life in Amsterdam; they gave me a more concrete sense of the place I lived in. Now, more than ever, they helped me to navigate it.

I looked around: Dario and Amir, Linda and Tessel, graphic designers, most of them, seemed to be taking sides passionately on some controversial topic or another. On the balcony were Iris, Saskia and Wayne. Zahra and Arno, both architects, were speaking with Väinö whom I had convinced to come. I skimmed the room but neither Emil nor Sofija had arrived yet, if they would be coming at all.

A small group made of Praneet, Cecilia and Alexander had been browsing the latest catalogue of Marlene Dumas's recent exhibition and seemed to be discussing it. I sensed the intoxication in their voices; the cocktails loosening tongues and relaxing minds. What could the silence of Sofija and Emil mean? She had mentioned that she was seeing him this week. She might have told him, then, about last Sunday. I had suggested to each of them separately that they come together to the party. But after what had happened, I wasn't sure that Emil would show up.

At that precise moment, they made their entrance, together, looking very much like a couple, down to their matching outfits of white shirts and sleek trousers. Sofija was glowing and I immediately felt a twinge of jealousy seeing her arm in arm with a very smug-looking Emil. Thankfully it was Anton who greeted them and steered them towards Marcus at the bar. I circulated in the other room for a bit, and observed them from a distance, as they spoke with Floris, and then Sofija went on to introduce Emil to artists she had worked with.

He kept her close to him, milling around her or standing nearby, affecting a detached air, while his hand hovered around her waist or his arm demonstratively wrapped itself around her shoulders. I heard him laugh once or twice. It rang a little fake, I thought. His display of overconfidence looked painfully as if it was compensating for something. I recognised it, having seen it once or twice before. They had moved on and were chatting with Akwasi and Cassie. As I approached their group, I sensed a nervousness, even hostility in the way Emil began to speak, eyes turned firmly away from me.

Only later did Sofija come towards me, alone. She brushed my shoulder lightly, and at the touch of her body I felt a tingle. I expected our bodies to melt and merge into one again. I was about to follow her somewhere quiet, anywhere, but she just stopped and whispered into my ear.

'I told him about Sunday just before we came. That's why we are late – and in matching outfits. He was furious, mind you.' She looked at me with a perfectly innocent pout and continued:

'I hadn't anticipated that, somehow.' She stepped back, a slight mocking smile on her face, and walked away. Emil was putting up a fine show. Sofija seemed more to be her usual self, or what I knew of it, motioning around the crowd, falling into conversations with one bunch of people and then another. I enjoyed looking at her as she walked lightly around the house. It made our afternoon in her bed seem more tangible, however much she affected a detached look when our gazes met. I heard her husky laugh a few times. I wanted her to feel embraced by the food, the flowers, the congenial atmosphere. To feel my care for her. If only Emil could stop touching her all the time. I could not imagine she enjoyed being paraded in that way, as one half of a couple. The smug, closed face he put on suddenly made his usual neediness all the more contemptible.

I walked as far away from him as I could, onto the balcony where David was holding court. He interrupted his story to praise the food and bring me up to speed with the conversation, and then resumed his exposé about governmental art policies as Adelia and Floris listened. I sat around with them for a while, looking at the pink blueish sky over the rooftops at the back of the courtyard.

The energy of the beginning of the evening had given way to a quieter mellowness. It was not going to be a very late night, on a weekday, but people seemed in no hurry to leave, just yet. The air became cooler and people began to step inside and close the pairs of French windows that led to the balconies at both ends of the flat. Most of them were Anton's friends, really, but then, who really counted for me in Amsterdam? Anton's nicer colleagues, perhaps, mine at the Covert, probably, a handful of artists I had met over the years. But most of my dearest friends apart from Cassie lived abroad, in Paris or London. I was not sure I could have lived here all these years without her. Earlier Victor had announced he was going to bed and Cassie had gone up with him. Now I saw her checking the food and drinks for anything that needed to be cleared away. Sofija and Emil seemed to have vanished. Probably all for the best.

The evening was settling in and we lit candles around the house. The discussion became more muted. Akwasi seemed to be getting intimate with Janis, a Californian photographer who was spending a semester in residency at the Covert Foundation. Citing kids and babysitters, a few people began to leave, but others, childless or parents to older kids, stuck around looking for more wine and gathering around the candles.

I withdrew onto the sofa, curled up in one of its corners and looked around at the small clusters of people speaking in hushed tones as the impassive voice of Lou Reed singing on *Transformer* filled the space. Väinö was still around, leaning against a wall in the next room, speaking with a Finnish textile artist he had spent the best part of the evening with. Earlier, when he was lending me a hand to clear up empty plates, he whispered he was happy to be there although the invitation had startled him at first. He was nervous about meeting Anton and being in my house, of being introduced to my other life. But now, he said, he was 'absolutely fine, really nice to be here,' he nodded, as the slight hiss of his accent made 'nice' sound particularly delicious. Beautiful, charming Väinö, whom I had met in the first weeks of my February dating spree, was one of the very few in the house tonight who had anything to do with what my life had really been about in the past months.

Conversations appeared to dwindle until they blurred into little more than indistinct murmurs. I looked around drowsily and I imagined for a moment that all the men I had slept with this year had joined the party. Heiko, predictably, would be over there mixing cocktails. Timo, the software guy, would be entertaining David with his knowledge of algorithms. Arnold would be surveying the street from the balcony and, I could imagine him vividly, would be drowning gallerists with questions about market trends, and enjoying the company of artists next to whom he would feel something of an artist too. I visualized them for a moment drinking cocktails and sampling the food. Armana, the Kenyan businessman, would be exchanging notes about prospects in the global art economy with Cassie, charming her with his touchy-feely attitude. Stefan, savvy as always, would be holding court, like David did, and explaining in his over-elaborate vocabulary the ins and outs of the German theatre world to Anton, who was fascinated by all things German. As a long-running joke, the Italian guy would make an appearance, clutching his usual sports bag as he stood at the door. Or perhaps, better, he would be with his wife, this time. They would all be talking and laughing, as they would mingle seamlessly with other guests.

I looked around the room again, but the reality was that only Väinö, Sofija and Emil, bridged my family and my other life. All the others belonged to a concealed, secret, second life, my space outside of domesticity and marriage, and for that very reason they would never taste my cooking or be welcome in my home.

And yet, those were the people with whom I had lived some of the most intense moments of the last eight months, the most exciting adventures, the most powerful experiences. Moments when I had truly been myself. Several of them had become little more than just a name, or an address: however hard I tried to remember their faces, to conjure up a hair colour, the shade and texture of skin, nothing more came to mind. Still, they were part of that story.

A jumble of details came hurtling back. The softness of someone's lips, the colour of the sheets on a bed, the joyful, peaceful or lugubrious atmosphere of a house, the squeak-iness of the leather on a sofa. I remembered hands holding their hardened cocks, and of being in someone's arms. The delicious shiver down the spine when a hand slipped under my top or my skirt, and when a hand pulled off my tights. Those faint images and faded sensations made up my real map of the city. The network of people and addresses thanks to which I could now orientate myself, find my place in Amsterdam.

I remembered small flats in improbable neighbourhoods, even smaller ones perched under the roofs of seventeenth-century merchant houses; flats in nineteenth-century workers' houses with paper-thin walls, in brand new high-rises in the business district, in art deco housing estates near the Mercatorplein. I remembered hairy and hairless torsos, skinny feet sticking out of duvets, coffees being stirred ner-vously in bars, and glasses of water thirstily downed after sex. I remembered being undressed and dressing up again, looking for underwear in the folds of the sheets, feeling light-headed and noticing my voice had become husky after too much shouting.

Those fragments, bits and scraps of life were indelible even as the rest of those meetings fell into oblivion. They felt more real, more pregnant at any rate than the artist studios I had visited, the reports I had typed up, the meetings I had attended, some weekends spent with Victor and Anton, the articles I had written and the books I had read.

Those intimate experiences were the things that made the hairs on the back of my arms rise and sent shivers down the small of my back as I remembered them sitting in the living room at the end of my party. That was my real life, half clandestine perhaps, but one that really mattered. I had been more intimate with these men whose names I could not all remember than with the people who had come to the party.

I could be making dinner or helping Victor to tidy his room, and be mentally composing answers to messages or planning what to wear for a date the next day. I seldom kept a trace of those exchanges, the ones that stayed in my head for hours, the ones that demanded a light touch and could, at every answer, turn one way or the other. They disappeared each time I had deleted the app. The slate was clean, and I could start afresh once again, vivified by this form of amnesia that gave me the illusion that anything could happen, that nothing had happened yet. And each time I deleted the app, I knew that the few awkward exchanges and unpleasant discussions that it also contained would simply go away. Until I was ready to restore my profile, that life receded into the shadows and I could turn fully to my other life: pick up files and Lego pieces and email editors and artists. But who could say which of those two lives was more real? Who could say that those personal and professional attachments, built over the years in face-to-face exchanges, were truer and more durable, more important than the ones built digitally and that vanished at the press of a button?

Each one of those lives existed side by side, rhymed by their own rituals and habits. I looked at the remnants of the evening for which I had chosen flowers, collected recipes and thought up dishes for weeks on end before the party. And then planning, shopping, cooking, tidying up, laying out, pulling out platters from cupboards that were too high for me, setting out the buffet, thinking of napkins and cutlery and glasses. In those moments, I more or less consciously channelled the perfect hostess my mother had always been, the one who made her kids politely greet the guests and pass hors d'oeuvres round to them before disappearing to bed without making a fuss about her absence at our bedside for a last goodnight kiss. Like her, I wore lipstick and planned things, down to leaving the table in the middle of the room so that, if the party became too crowded, a couple of friends would help move it to the side. Even the spontaneity was planned, perfectly orchestrated: 'So many people came that we had to push the table against the wall.'

Next to those rituals were other, more intimate ones that mirrored them. They included showering, shaving and moisturising before going out on a date, choosing clothes and rummaging through drawers for matching underwear. It was about embodying a certain idea of femininity, wearing perfume and nail polish. I remembered now, in disbelief, how I had gone to my first two dates wearing high heels. The very thought of it made me cringe now, and yet I still made sure I was smooth-skinned and delicately scented. It made things feel safer on the surface, it disguised insecurities.

The two routines paralleled one another, and save for exceptions carefully thought through, they needed to remain carefully separated. No wonder I had been shocked when Jonas, 'the man who hid his condoms', had come knocking at the door, preceded by two cheerful boys, one of whom was my son.

'Goodbye darling, thanks for the great party! And it was great to speak with you Monday. I have thought about all this some more. Can we speak tomorrow?' David's syrupy voice interrupted me. He had slid onto the sofa besides me, raincoat flung over his arm, chirruping into my ear. I stirred, looked at him uncomprehending for a minute. 'Yes,' I murmured. 'Tomorrow, of course, thank you for coming tonight.'

•

I didn't hear from Emil or Sofija for a few days after the party. I had nothing more to say to Emil, and was sure he had sensed, that evening, that his mere presence exasperated me. But I yearned for Sofija's body, for the smooth way that she moved around and communicated what she wanted.

Finally, she texted me. She wanted to speak about Emil, to show me something. Could I meet her near her office for a quick lunch?

I walked into Restaurant As before she arrived. It was housed in a brutalist circular building nested between other modernist constructions and flanking the Beatrix Park, just outside the perimeter of the business district adjacent to Zuid Station. Inside, the atmosphere was Scandinavian, with long tables of rough wood that radiated from the centre, with white rugs and pastel-coloured cushions on the benches. She had booked a small table in a side booth, between two radial supporting walls that framed a bay window with a view onto the park. Her usual table, I understood. As I sat down, I saw her arrive. She smiled and nodded to the waiter and her bangs revealed her forehead for a brief instant. She walked around the room like a diva taking to the stage in this radical decor, circling the long tables placed like helixes around a central axis, until she reached me, preceded by her smoky incense scent.

She let her coat slip off her shoulders onto the bench, then grabbed a pink cushion to sit on.

'Do you know this place?' This was where she came almost every day when she had work lunches, she said.

'It dates from the late 1950s, and was part of a cloister. I always feel there is something quite spiritual about the place.' She looked around briefly and then, without as much as a glance towards the menu, she waved down a waiter and ordered the regular lunch board for two: cold cuts and roast vegetables and greens.

'It's their best thing, you will see.' A twinkle in her eyes.

I searched for the outline of her breasts under the silky fabric of the blouse, looked at her face for an expression of softness, a sign she remembered our last lunch and what it had led to.

'You look amazing! I like these pussy bow shirts on you. Tell me: how are you? How have you have been?'

She was bent over her phone, a shield against our intimacy, scrolling down the screen. She looked up, distractedly.

'I've been good, work is seriously picking up, though ... crazy at the moment, with all the fairs coming up ...' Barely glancing at me, eyes back on the phone. Now she looked up at me, serious.

'So, thank you for coming. I can't take very much time off work, and I know that you are busy too, but I thought it was much better that we do this together. In short, Emil has just been horrible to me since our ... lunch ... and even more so since the party. I know he hasn't spoken to you but he is very upset. He feels we have two-timed him. He thinks it is all your doing.'

'Which is ridiculous,' I interrupted, smiling. 'I distinctly remember how you began to undress me ...'

Her face lit up.

'It was a beautiful afternoon. But he thinks your history – your dating history, I mean – is reason enough to believe that it is you who made the first move. He says he does not trust me anymore. But I, I am not sure I can really trust him either. I would like to check a few dates and facts with you, if that's OK?'

We put our phones side by side and scrolled through weeks of messaging, patiently going through the chronology of the story we had shared, unknowingly for her.

'That Emil assured me that you and he were finished together when you were not ... at the very time that you were demanding honesty and transparency from him ... That just throws me, I had to see it for myself, thank you.'

She almost whispered this, as she pointed out dates when she wondered where he was and he had been with me. And then I understood that those days where he had been emotionally absent and physically exhausted were the days that he had spent with her and had been unable to say so, however much I had asked him to be open and honest.

She then told me about her exchange with Emil after that Sunday, and then ever since the party.

'He behaved in such a macho and possessive way when he heard that we had slept together, like you were another guy competing with him. He was perfectly ridiculous. He sensed a threat coming from you, it seems. It was like you had the balls, all along, and he was only just understanding that.'

She had confronted him over his lies, his dismissal of our ongoing affair at the time when they had met. I was glad that she had made similar requests of honesty from him. They had broken up in the end. The falling out, following the mistrust, had been so strong that it eased the pain, she said.

'I think that we were both taken for a ride, that in the end Emil is all smoke and mirrors. He gives off the appearance of someone creative and confident, but that hides a desperate attempt at self-improvement that comes out of, I think, a deep lack of self-confidence. Don't you think? He seems to think that if the self-branding is right, then the rest will follow, people will trust him, clients will flock to him, along with girlfriends. And, my God, his thing about typography was so annoying. Did he also show you his collection of all that' – she gestured in the air – 'stuff?'

I smiled. I wished I could have taken Sofija to the park outside the restaurant, and then to the Citizen M hotel across the street with its immaculate tiny rooms and wide beds. I wished I could have made love with her and that she would let me caress her and replay the afternoon in her bedroom. Instead of that, she became more professional again, smooth-talking, asked for the bill, and soon said goodbye. She needed time to think. I looked at her walking away.

•

As before, her message was short, to the point. I had not heard from Sofija in weeks. I had answered immediately, with clammy palms. Of course, yes, I would come by. She was working from home today.

I barely registered the traffic on the short ride to her place. She was waiting for me at the top of her stairs, a teasing look in her eyes, in a slouchy T-shirt and matching trousers, and walked barefoot around her flat. She was sorry for the long silence, she had been so busy. She kissed me lightly on the lips, and I felt instantly a wetness between my legs. I followed her into the kitchen.

'Coffee?'

I nodded and patted my pocket. The phone was whirring. As I reached to switch it off, I noticed a couple of calls, missed while I was cycling. Unknown number.

'Do pick up, I'll make the coffee.'

At first, I didn't quite understand the woman speaking in Dutch. 'Victor,' she said in an urgent tone. And then ... 'schuur'. I repeated the word, uncomprehendingly, in front of Sofija. 'Ziekenhuis'. Hospital. 'What? Could you speak English, please?' The voice continued in Dutch, repeating the words. 'Victor', 'schuur', 'ziekenhuis'. I broke into a cold sweat and handed the phone over to Sofija.

'Please ... I don't understand.'

Sofija introduced herself and listened for a few minutes,

frowning. I tried to get her attention: 'What happened, where is he?' She raised her free hand to silence me and turned away, asked a few questions I did not understand. She finished the call.

'OK, stay calm. Victor's been hurt. He has banged his head.' She fiddled with her phone. I stared at her.

'They say he went very white, and he is bleeding. They couldn't figure out if he had passed out or not, so they've taken him to hospital, in case he has a concussion.' The blood drained from my face. Before I was able to say anything, she continued,

'It doesn't sound too bad, really. But they weren't able to reach you or Anton, so someone from school has taken him to the AMC hospital. You need to go there now.' She tapped away at her phone again, unemotional. 'I'm getting you an Uber. There. Four minutes.'

At the hospital they insisted that I first register him as a patient. I wanted to see him. The schuur, what the hell was that? The receptionist asked for Victor's insurance card. I tried to explain it was in Anton's wallet. In Düsseldorf, with Anton. She raised an eyebrow and switched to English.

'Do you know the name of Victor's huisarts? Huisarts? You call them GP?'

I raked my brain. Verhaast? Verhulst? Verhaven? I hopelessly tapped into my phone. Maybe I'd made a note of it somewhere.

'He is on his father's insurance,' I tried to explain. 'His father is the one who takes him to the doctor.' The receptionist did not seem impressed.

'Can you show me anything? His passport, maybe?'

'He was born here!' I finally blurted. 'Victor van Dijk! You must have a record of him in your files. He was born right here, on the fifth floor, 22 December 2004!'

The receptionist's attitude changed immediately. 'Ah then, that makes it easier. Victor is at home here.' She smiled and tapped away at her computer. 'There, I have him in the system. Please follow the letter B down that way. Room 14A.'

They had just finished putting in the stiches as I walked in. The school staff had left. Victor lay there, on the examination table, motionless.

The nurse greeted me. 'You're Victor's mother? We had to put in a few stiches. But the cut's not so deep. We've given him a light sedative. He is a little groggy.'

I walked up to him. His eyes were closed. I felt my throat constrict. 'Concussion?' I murmured.

'No, no concussion.' The nurse walked out of the curtained area. I looked at Victor's limp skinny body. He looked so small, so frail, on the blue examination table. Anything could have happened. I hadn't been there for him. His breathing was regular under the soft features. Colour seemed to return slowly to his cheeks. A few hairs were caught in the bandage that barred his forehead. He opened his eyes.

I held him tight against me during the taxi ride home. Modern high-rise office blocks gave way to mid-century brick apartment buildings; it was the same route I had taken almost a decade earlier when he was born, stunned and proud of the small creature swaddled in white, lodged in my arms. We had never been back there together in all this time. Victor perked up a little on the ride, looking out of the window dozily.

I finally managed to get Anton on the phone and Victor, now seemingly fully recovered, recounted the whole running game that had ended with him racing straight into the sharp corner of the playground shed. The 'schuur', as he repeated to his dad. The shock of the collision seemed to have subsided. I made a picnic dinner that we ate together in bed.

'Do you think Daddy would be OK with us eating in his bed? Are you really *really* sure I can sleep in your bed?' I wasn't prepared to let him out of my sight for a second. Victor was delighted the end of the day had turned into a pyjama party in the big bed. He fell asleep in my arms, watching his favourite Miyazaki cartoon. As I listened to his smooth breathing, I thought about the events of the day, from Sofija's message that had made me forget about everything, to Anton's absence. And then my shortcomings: losing the little Dutch I knew in the panic, and why didn't I have all that information that any normal mother would have somewhere? Because that was Anton's department? Really? Was I kidding myself? Anything could have happened to Victor.

Sofija had sent flowers and a Tintin card for Victor who had asked me who this friend was. Anton had played down the incident, as had the school. They were practical, efficient. Like Sofija, who had been so helpful. Accidents happen, they said. Victor, in the weeks that followed, would say, eyes twinkling, that he had fallen off Totoro's big belly. Only I seemed to be shaken, days on, about my failings, about the memory of my son lying motionless on the examination table, about the receptionist's perplexed look as I fumbled with doctor's names. Weeks later, I had not heard back from Sofija after my last messages to her. I had been dismissed. A faulty catch with too much baggage.

11

Dissonant

I had set the dating app to show me profiles of 'only women'. There were so many fewer cards to go through that I had expanded the age range from thirty to sixty years old. Was that why what I saw was so disconcerting? Whereas the men shared a few standard poses and contexts – fishing, running, sitting in bars and restaurants, sitting next to blurred-out women and holding small children or dogs – the repertory of gestures and backdrops of women was far wider. There were older women wearing plaid shirts open onto T-shirts and sporting salt-and-pepper buzz cuts, and there were androgynous women in their twenties. But there were also women in their thirties dressed in low-cut, revealing tops or high-split skirts that I would have thought belonged to the heterosexual-only seduction panoply. Several women on the app defined themselves as queer, others were bi-curious, they explained, and a few noted deep down in their profile text that they were hoping to meet a woman for a threesome with their male partner, someone who would be up for 'a fun and daring date'.

I swiped more slowly. Women's profile pictures seemed to be framed somewhat differently than men's photographs. There were far fewer sunglasses, and more expressive faces, as if personality here trumped physical attributes and life-style. There were fewer pets also, no babies, and nobody posed with drumkits or motorbikes between their legs. But then occasionally, some pictures looked like they were directed at men: women posed in front of mirrors, in high heels and pouting lips, or even in swimsuits. Each time, I paused swiping; trying to decide if this was some lesbian code I did not get or if they had fully internalized the male gaze. Perhaps they had just accidentally ticked the 'show me to women' box.

I had been brought up to know the rules of heterosexual sex, I had learnt to show my body in certain contexts, to protect it in others and to make it available at prearranged moments only. As a little girl I was told how to behave or rather to 'be good', to like certain things more than others. I had been taught to not scream too loud and not flash my knickers when I climbed trees, to brush my hair and pull up my socks. But as far as I could remember, I felt like I had never encountered any obstacle, or ever thought that a career or personal aspiration was out of reach because I was a woman, hence my late awakening to feminism. This was the argument that Simone de Beauvoir had once used to explain why she had not addressed feminist issues earlier than in *The Second Sex,* and I gladly borrowed it from her.

Looking at those pictures of women showing cleavage and pouting lips I understood why the women with buzz cuts and plaid shirts seemed so inaccessible and mysterious to me. The way I had learnt to decode the world was as a guest, as an 'other' as Beauvoir wrote, taught to groom myself and behave in relation to a masculinity that was the default, central position. When I had asked it to show profiles of men, the app had presented me a kind of doubling of the world outside, a caricature of testosterone that was, if anything, a rosy vision of a sunnier and plentiful world. Now, as it showed women, it revealed a more secretive underside that did not match with the world I had grown up in. Perhaps it was because this heterosexual norm had been so deeply ingrained in my brain that I had felt rejected in those lesbian bars. Each image on the app was a puzzle made of words and images that masked an individual story I wanted to know. Each belonged to a woman I had met a hundred times on the street and yet that I had never seen, a woman who conformed to an idea of womanhood and yet at the same time rearranged, questioned, tinkered with that idea and subverted it.

●

I would have liked to discuss all this with Sofija. I thought I could understand now what those words she had said at the end of our first meeting in her house, that she was not bisexual, had really meant. I wanted to tell her I understood, now, the complexity she had revealed, something of it, at least. But when I thought of her, it was the image of her on the phone to the hospital that stuck; the frowning that had made my blood run cold, her arm raised to keep me quiet, and the moment she explained that Victor had had an accident. She had dealt with it; and now she was blanking me. Things were so hectic at work, she said in short, carefully worded messages. There was the art fair in Paris, and then Frieze in London and then Art Basel Miami. She hoped Victor, Anton and I were doing well. I had tried weeks later; the events were different, but the answer was the same.

Now and then, I walked by her house and looked up at the balcony outside of her living room. From a certain spot in the park below I could make out the sofa, and even more vaguely the colour of the curtains around the window. Nothing more. I had forgotten what colour they were, if I had ever noticed it in the first place. But I wasn't sure. The lights in her flat only went on late in the day, I noticed that when I managed to pass by, running an errand in her neighbourhood timed precisely before the shops closed, but when she might just be back at home. I never saw her in the street, never ran into her at openings, or had done so only once or twice at large events where she was, as always, surrounded by her posse of suitable suited men and engaged in conversations. Our meeting had broken all the routines and the customs I had established since February. She was the only person I had had sex with, since then, whom I had not met on the internet. She wasn't a profile I could delete, or swipe right or left. She wasn't even a waifish young man to whom I could explain in plain words this was a passing thing. She was a woman I had known, and who had known me, by sight, for years. Having severed ties with Emil and with no news from Sofija, I had crawled back to the safe tangibility of the digital world.

At least I had believed that until I had begun to look for

women. I did not expect to see Sofija on the dating app; especially as she had, in one of her rare text messages, mentioned there was a new man in her life. But still, I longed to experience again something of that sensuality, that pleasure, that independence and that calm that I had felt in her arms. Eventually, I had tried out sending a few messages to these women who were all mysteries, and I had ended up going for a few inconclusive coffees and drinks. I came on fast, unsubtly, I realized after each meeting.

When I tried to visualize myself, I saw a burly middle-aged man hunched over a drink, making unsubtle innuendos, and methodically cornering the woman in front of me to get to where I wanted. The image of Timo, the thick-set software engineer who lived in the Meander, came back. I thought of his square shoulders under the oversized jacket, of his bald head, and pictured myself with similarly exaggerated shoulders under an ill-fitting jacket, bent over my single malt, smugly explaining the algorithm to some unexperienced young woman who would be trying to play it cool. I had 'come on strong', as he would have perhaps put it to his flatmate, with a young Indian woman I had drunk a Coke with, at a hotel bar one afternoon. She was thin-boned and smart, with an ironic gaze and tumbling black hair, and I had failed to understand her subtle recoiling from my advances. In the end she had just spelt it out, flatly: she was categorically not interested in meeting again. She had an engineer husband, and she was just curious about the world of women who love women. She wanted to know more, to be titillated over a drink but nothing else. I had felt like a total fool.

I had repeated this absurd experience with some variations not long after one evening at Café de Pels, with a Dutch
woman in her mid-fifties. She stumbled into the bar, all
brown boots, straggly hair and bright red lipstick that bled
at the corners of her mouth. She looked ill at ease, eyes dart-
ing around the room, as she dumped an overflowing bucket
handbag onto the coarse wood table. This time it was her
who had been abrupt, asking me my favourite sexual games
with women and mocking me for being taken aback. She had
sarcastically commented on my ignorance, explaining that
scissoring was her thing and I could just google it if I had
no idea what that was. Two beers later, she had admitted,
dramatically, that she had never slept with a woman and that
she had to go home immediately, alone, to finish doing her
laundry. She had practically run away after that awkward
outpouring. I wished I had done exactly that.

I was seriously considering taking a break when I had been
approached by Olivia, a Canadian geography professor who
had been spending a couple of months in Amsterdam doing
research and was soon going back to Bristol. She was relaxed
and great fun when we met for a drink. She was thrilled to
be in Amsterdam, and her first stop in the city had been for
the Homomonument on the Westermarkt. But lesbian bars
weren't her thing. She had a short sabbatical to write up
research she'd done here, about the polders and peat, and
knew Botshol like the back of her hand. It felt good to speak
about the UK with someone. She was staying in an Airbnb
rental, one of a succession of places, and chose each one in a
different area of Amsterdam so as to sample the atmosphere

and meet some locals. She offered to take me back to the houseboat she lived on at the moment. It was a fabulous place, she enthused, with a couple of cats she had to take care of. The deck was covered with dozens of potted plants, and it was moored on the Prinseneiland, the most beautiful of the Westelijke Eilanden, the three islands around which Amsterdam had been built in the seventeenth century. I tried to block out her gaudy earrings and mum jeans and followed her to the houseboat.

The deck looked directly on to one of the old double drawbridges that served as entryways onto the island: the Drieharingbrug; the bridge of the three herrings. I knew someone who lived around there, a colleague from the Covert Foundation. At work, Wietske told us stories about the congregations of cats that roamed the old shipyards, and of the communal atmosphere created by the diehard Amsterdammers that were her neighbours. Many of them were ex-hippies who, following in the footsteps of the artists and musicians who had begun to repopulate the uninhabited island after the war years, had settled in this quiet, secretive island in the centre of the city.

Olivia laid out her lesbian credentials with the same heavy-handedness as I had played the burly macho. She told me about the sexual education she had received in the feminist lesbian circles in San Francisco when she was a student, and said she had timed the beginning of her research trip to coincide with the Amsterdam Gay pride. She had been amazed by the hundreds of boats on the canals, the large official ones and the small motorboats that followed and accompanied them and the crowds clad in white, pink and rainbow flags that cheered from the banks.

'How do you like using Airbnb?' I asked conversationally as she preceded me down a narrow staircase to the main room of the boat.

'It's been amazing to live in all these different parts of town.' Before the houseboat she had lived near the Dappermarkt, the old Surinamese neighbourhood where gentrification could be observed on a daily basis. She had also spent time in one of those ultra-modern high-rises near the Lloyd Hotel, in the old dockyards.

'I feel like I've seen a lot in, what, a month and a half? Almost two months.'

She surveyed the low-ceilinged space we had descended into, a living room crammed with books, vintage furniture and faded rugs that opened onto a spacious kitchen with large windows.

'This one is the most interesting in terms of space. Never lived on a boat before. Have you?'

'No. Doesn't it feel strange to be amidst other people's things? I don't know if I would like that.'

'Well, it is true that this particular place is very lived in, but in others, people make everything personal disappear in a locked room or something and they make their place look like it could be anywhere, a bit sterile. But no, I really like it. It feels more informal than being in a rental place. Or a hotel.'

I smiled encouragingly. 'In any case it is very special to see Amsterdam from water level. I haven't seen it that way very often.' Bookcases framed a single long horizontal window that looked out to the other side of the canal with its ancient warehouses turned into lofts.

Olivia offered me another whisky and we chatted a little longer as the light went down. I was expecting her to make a move, to kiss me, gradually wondering if maybe she only wanted a drinking partner for the night. I hesitated and then, getting up from the sofa as if to observe the water, I walked up to her and ruffled her soft, babylike hair over the hideous looped earrings.

'May I kiss you?' Instead of answering she lifted her head up and gave me a hungry, wet, long kiss.

'Come,' she murmured, 'I'll show you the bedroom.' She pointed to a closed door at the bow of the boat. Framed by two porthole windows, the bed was a kind of wide berth that occupied most of the cabin-like room.

She kissed me as she pressed me down onto the bed, pulled up my skirt and dragged my underwear down my legs.

'Ooh, now, that's a very pretty pussy,' she exclaimed, lightly stroking my pubic hair. I could not believe anyone was speaking to me like that. If it had been a man, I would have instantly told him to get lost. But it felt so good when she began to rub my cunt that I set her patronising ways aside, and said nothing more until I began to moan. She did not allow me a single gesture towards her as she continued to tease, rub and lick me expertly. I came instantly, repeatedly, shouting and shivering as I felt her fingers and tongue stimulating precisely the clit and the softer area at the opening of the vagina, and rubbing them continuously. My voice became coarser, but there seemed to be nothing I could do. Each time

I tried to touch her she would push me away. She made sure I was her thing and that her own body stayed firmly off limits.

I looked up and around, in the bedroom alcove, while Olivia continued to savour me, and caught the faces of the happy family in the framed pictures surrounding the bed. They had no idea, that anonymous family, of what was happening in the Airbnb, and it felt strange to share that moment of intimacy with strangers. I closed my eyes as I felt another orgasm pushing its way from my lower abdomen to the breast she was kneading with her free hand. I opened them and wondered about this intimacy that we shared with others on the dating app and now on Airbnb, as other framed photos of laughing children came into my visual field. And then my eyes fell on a portrait I wished immediately I could have unseen: Wietske, from accounting. Damn! Wietske from the Covert Foundation, with a big grin on her face, standing next to her husband while I was having sex with a woman in her bed! Their kids were beaming in dozens of pictures around the room. I could just imagine how uncomfortable I would feel sitting across her in the next foundation meeting.

'Stay for the night, why don't you,' Olivia purred, as we lay next to one another chatting, later on.

'I am not sure . . . I might have to go home . . . my son wakes up early . . . But it's so good to be here, maybe I can stay a little longer,' I whispered.

'If you don't want to stay overnight then I would prefer you leave right now, actually. I really need my sleeping hours.'

I recoiled at Olivia's reply and awkwardly gathered my things. I repeated her words to myself on a loop as I cycled

home, stunned as much by her brutal treatment as by the
smiling face of Wietske in the photograph. Both remained
firmly imprinted in my head, many weeks later.

●

Efrat, I quickly realized, also had a thing about being
touched. It had to be done on her own terms, she had been
specific about it from the outset. I had met her a week or so
after the peculiar evening with Olivia who had disappeared
soon after our meeting. Wietske was back in the office, beaming from her little holiday, and without a word about having
rented out her houseboat during her absence. I almost asked
her, once or twice, if she knew about Airbnb, just to see if she
would mention Olivia, but didn't. But for a few days, whenever I saw Wietske in the office I felt a sharp tingle on my clit
and remembered lying spreadeagled in her bed.

I had matched almost inadvertently with Efrat late one
evening, when I was in bed, by myself, absent-mindedly
swiping while reading a book. We had chatted a little,
exchanging book titles – she was also in bed, reading and
swiping, she said, and it had been an easy enough exchange
until she had explained she was an artist, a painter, on a
residency program in Amsterdam. Her last words stopped
me in my tracks. After the Olivia/Wietske experience, after
Emil and Sofija, I wanted to keep the dating app as separate
as I could from the rest of my life.

I tried to get out of the conversation, to cut her short and
unmatch her. I began to answer her in monosyllables, then
stayed silent for an hour or so. She sent me another message,

and then I realized that I would inevitably run into her some
time or another in the Amsterdam art world. I finally told
her about the kind of work I did with artists, about my job at
the foundation, and proposed to meet the following Monday
morning just after nine for a coffee at a busy, businesslike
place. That would be an absolute deterrent to anything happening between us. The discussion about art foundations and
artist residencies continued when we met. We spoke over the
noise of the coffee machines and the comings and goings of
morning regulars chatting with the barista or tapping away
at their phones while they waited to be served. She inquired
about funding possibilities from the Covert and told me
about her residency. The shop talk made me cringe but she
was beautiful, with her matt skin, green eyes and curly dark
hair. She was intense and guarded, much more than I was.

I was mollified by her attitude and offered to meet again, in
the evening, at café Brecht, a deep and narrow place hidden
on the Weteringschans, chock-full of vintage armchairs and
furniture with walls covered in faded flowery paper and a
gleaming wooden bar top that ran the length of the room.
It was busy with students, mostly, although I saw Arnold at
a distance. He approached; we exchanged a few words and
I introduced them. When he left, she had a mysterious grin
on her face.

'So, this is the kind of boy you sleep with? Did you see
the look on his face? I can tell he wants more of you ...
Maybe I should tell him that he is too late, and that we have
other plans!'

She took me back to the small studio she had been

allocated by the Dutch-Israeli foundation that was funding her stay. It was in one of those former warehouses on the Brouwersgracht, the 'brewers' canal' that had been built in the early seventeenth century for the city's merchants. Its vernacular architecture gave the canal a more subdued atmosphere than the gabled mansions elsewhere, and when we cycled there, the waterways were lit with the orange glow of lamp posts. We kissed on the canal and made love by the windows, looking at the dark, opaque water below. She was reserved and precise in her gestures, quietly persuasive, slow, firm. She pushed me away when I was too forward, enacted limits that were not, as with Olivia, about power games and controlling. I felt a fragility, a caution that I could only respect. She was in all ways the opposite of the sexy, extravagant and once promiscuous Sofija.

After that first evening, I returned many times to the Brouwersgracht. She told me what to do, encouraged me. She glided above and under my body expertly, sliding her hand inside me and making my body open up, making the wetness invade everywhere, and letting me be submerged by sensations of weightlessness and drifting. Occasionally she let me taste her, but never opened up completely. I caressed the rough, grainy skin of her thighs, and the bushy pubic hair. Hers was a woman's body that was not groomed, polished, painted and plucked for the touch of a man. My mostly hairless body, soft and moisturized skin, my painted nails brought a lenient smile to her face.

'Do you always shave like that? Do you feel the need? Or is it the boys . . . ?'

When she asked, I looked at my skin and saw years of grooming that I had been taught were necessary in order to become an object desire on the part of the opposite sex. When she ran her short fingers and tiny hands across my skin, I realized I didn't need to scrub it with such determination, that all that scrubbing and polishing, all that getting rid of the blemishes, of the tiny asperities on its surface, was also a gesture of self-erasure.

After sex, we spoke – or rather, most often, she spoke – wrapped in each other's arms in her narrow bed. She often told me, then, about her childhood in Israel.

'In the kibbutz, we all grew up in the children's house, we were raised together by all the parents in the community. It is hard to understand how much that experience shapes your perception of society. But that's why I always feel a bit different. You learn to take your own place amidst the other kids, you are taught that your needs or desire are just as important or unimportant as those of the next kid.'

She described the landscapes she grew up in, she explained the territorial struggles of the Palestinians, and how wars framed each period of her life growing up. She opposed the politics of her country, without renouncing it altogether. She wanted to move away, she said, yet felt shaped by that socialist utopia she had lived in her childhood and teens. She was free, and yet she wanted to have a child. I told her how that would change her, that she would never be alone. We spoke about Victor, of my wonder at seeing him grow into himself, from the exuberant toddler to the more serious little boy with strong opinions and preferences that he had recently become. I told her about his accident, weeks back, and how the sight of him helpless in the hospital bed had reminded me of how small he still was despite his aspirations to be more independent. It had reawakened that visceral worry for another living being that I had felt the moment he had been born.

I had never been to Israel, did not know anyone from there, save for distant family I never saw. Because I had not been raised in the faith, I had always thought that my Jewishness was limited to my cooking. And yet the things Efrat said, her gestures and attitudes, the intonations of her voice felt uncannily close; they resonated at some unspecified deeper level. Maybe it was that, physically, she looked like the women in my family. Or perhaps it was her singing accent, the Hebrew words she threw into the conversation, which I had heard from my parents. Being in her arms I felt we came from the same place, wherever that place might be. It was a homecoming. What I had at first taken for shyness was really a distance, a political engagement for the rights of gays, lesbians, and trans people that she led in an association in Tel Aviv, against the right-wing politicians, the ultra-orthodox and their pressure on state politics, and in everyday life.

All those things. The proximity we felt made it seem natural to bring her back home and introduce her to Anton. He liked her sensitivity and her vigilance. I think it reassured him that such a woman was my lover, rather than to see me fascinated by Sofija and entangled with Emil. Anton had never had any time for either of them, I realized, as I watched him speaking with Efrat. Sofija was part of his extended professional network, but with Efrat, Anton opened up about art, about politics and education for hours.

We shared quiet evenings at home with Anton and Victor who showed her his drawings. To our friends at dinner parties, she appeared to be a friend among others: our connection was invisible to them, while in the streets of Amsterdam, it was a new feeling to hold hands and to kiss as we did.

'I feel so free, bizarrely, as if I were another person.' I was giddy when I walked the streets of Amsterdam with her.

'But what you do not see is that you are safe here, to kiss me and to hold my hand. It's not something you can do everywhere.' She looked around.

'Do you mean in Israel?

'Yes, yes, in Israel, and in many other places in the world. In Israel you are safe in certain neighbourhoods of Tel Aviv, and you can hold hands there, but I don't do it. It is a complex society over there.'

With our friends, I noticed how she would often keep silent at first, observing each one's positions and postures and the things they referred to. Only after carefully gauging the context did she enter the conversation and make her point with surprising force. David adored her instantly, as did many others who commented that she and I looked as if we had always known one another.

When my parents visited for a weekend, ostensibly to see us, but really to spend time with Victor, they instantly took a shine to her. My father reminisced about his stay in a kibbutz in the late 1950s, and Efrat spoke in Hebrew with him. They embraced her without a question and I marvelled at the way she could play the perfect daughter and be a fiercely militant lesbian left-wing Israeli at the same time.

It was just like that. Efrat became part of my life. She did not attempt to highjack it, as Emil had done. She became a familiar presence amid my family and friends, no questions asked. Victor trusted her, and they spent time painting together. Our friendship was paired with an intense sexual connection that Anton knew about but never asked to be told about. When I was alone with her, I was amazed at the simplicity of our exchange and the way it moved fluidly from sex to conversation and back. We were intimate and straightforward together. The barrier of the opposite sex was absent, and with it, the urge to perform either the feminine or the masculine.

•

We had said our goodbyes when it was time for Efrat to return to Tel Aviv. She would be back, she said lightly. She had liked it all so much here in Amsterdam. No permanent war, no bombs, none of that tension that permeated life in Israel. The Foundation people were taking her to the airport. She did not like goodbyes. Neither did I. We joked about it and pretended that we would meet again very soon, a few months at most. But that night, in bed, I suddenly began to cry. Something poured out of me. Anton took me in his arms.

'I don't know why I am crying,' I repeated.

I did not understand it until he said the words.

'You are in love with her,' he whispered, holding me in the

dark. 'That's all. That's what it is. It is a beautiful thing. It will pass, so cherish it while it lasts.'

It felt strange hearing Anton saying those words, as if he was pointing out something so obvious yet that I was unable to see. Did I love her? Was I in love? I had no idea, but I knew that Efrat would stay in my life, somehow, that we had become part of one another.

I cried myself to sleep that night.

In the days and weeks that followed, Anton and I spoke more than we had for months. That night, when he had held me in bed as I cried, he had managed to put words to what I was experiencing better than I had been able to. He told me about Luciana, the Colombian architect, and how he had, for a moment, felt this attraction, how he had been under her spell, in awe and in love with her.

'I think you were so absorbed by your work then that I am not sure you noticed.'

I had not, but I had been preoccupied with other things.

'Yes, you worked a lot back then. I let it come over me like a wave. I knew it would not last, perhaps I felt that giddiness of new love for a month or two. I let it be. It was a sweet feeling. It should make you happy to have met someone like Efrat, someone so special.'

Then Anton reminded me how troubled I had looked that evening after the exhibition opening of Roni Horn, when I had followed him home, looking like I had seen a ghost.

'Yes, that was when I met Sofija.'

Anton pointed to the emotional rollercoaster I had put myself through these past months. I might have had at some point, I cautiously tried to explain, an obscure desire to seduce Sofija out of an impulse to compete with Emil, as a revenge for his encroachment onto my life.

'That was a macho trick you pulled. I don't think I or any of my male friends would have done something of the sort.'

'It wasn't just that, Anton. I wasn't just pulling a macho trick. There was something else. I thought Sofija was mesmerising. When I met her for lunch it was a bit as if those photographs of Renée Perle by Lartigue came to life. I showed them to you once: when I was a teenager, I tried to dress like those pictures. I identified with that woman. And then at lunch on the Amstel Sofija had suddenly brought those pictures to life. When the image of Sofija at the Ijsbreker came together with those photographs, it was like encountering a double of myself, a more beautiful and worldly double of myself.'

'It was something narcissistic ... that's what you are saying, isn't it?'

I let Anton's words hang there. There was so much more. it would take time to explain it, to unpack things. The adventure with Sofija had reshuffled the cards of my sexual identity, no less. But it would take some time to understand what that meant.

●

'Before then, before the whole thing with Sofija, before Emil even, there were moments you were simply not there with us, with Victor and me. There were times when I could see you looking for a refuge away from the stability of home, of us, when I sensed you craved instability, danger, chaos perhaps even?'

We were outside, on the pavement in front of the house, Anton tinkering with my bicycle, bent over the steering wheel. He repeatedly seemed to be unscrewing different pieces and putting them back, pulling the brakes apart and trying to understand what was wrong, muttering to himself and then, looking up, addressing me:

'I remember you constantly being on your phone, or just not showing interest in us. You didn't even come to the public lectures at the school anymore ...'

He interrupted his outpouring. He looked down at the fragments of the brakes scattered across a piece of cardboard, an obscure handful of small diverse objects.

He sighed: 'I am really not sure how to put this back together again ... It's a different kind of brakes from the ones on my own bike.'

'I think you saw I needed that chaos, that energy for a while. And then I found a quieter balance with Efrat.' I looked at him. 'I liked the intimacy we had, with her in our family. I just don't know how it will be now that she is gone; but I think I want things to be a little quieter, for us,' I said, not sounding as convincing as I'd hoped.

'I have been thinking about this since Victor's accident,' I went on. 'I have come a long way, longer than you think. When I spoke to Stefan, the German guy, about my depression after the pregnancy, when it all came back to me, those awful months after Victor was born. There was something else I did not tell you. I wanted to move out of the house, I needed some space. I know it is stupid, I see that now, but at the time, I feared that in order to find myself again I needed to leave our home and move away from you and him. I managed not to. Over time, I understood you were not to blame. But still, periodically, I feel this urge to take some distance, one way or the other. But I am back now.'

'Shit!'

Tiny screws tumbled onto the pavement.

'This is hopeless.' Anton sighed.

'Take a break, I will look for them. Have a cup of tea.' I handed him the flask.

Anton sat on the steps of our building and poured himself a mug of green tea, thoughtfully looking at the bicycle.

'I think I knew you wanted to leave, a long time ago, although I refused to see it. I felt it. But recently, it was different. You seemed to be absorbed in something. You fretted. I think it's this digital thing, this app, it stops you from seeing the world around you.'

'No!' I softened, 'No, that's not it. Maybe it got a little out of hand at some point. It's true it was so easy to just swipe and match and meet someone … Anyway, now I am looking at the world around me, and I can't see zilch!'

I peeled my eyes looking for the screws that had rolled around on the pavement, hiding under the small heaps of crinkly leaves.

'I mean,' Anton continued, 'those men and women you found on the app. You probably wouldn't have noticed them in real life, don't you think? Like they could pass by right now on the street and you would ignore them. Maybe you should stay off the app for good and try to do it the way I do it. Flirt with people in real life, people you might come across in bookstores or bars.'

I looked up, rolling a couple of screws between my fingers.

'But darling, that just does not happen anymore. It just doesn't. Most of the time it freaks people out, when a random stranger comes up to speak with them in a bookstore or a café.'

'I don't know. There is something really magical in spotting someone looking at you from the other end of a bar; to notice a woman across a room, and then to see her look back, to feel she responds to you, or initiates an exchange, without words. There is a connection at that precise moment, in a space filled with strangers. I love the way it just happens in the moment. You need to decide what to do, to act or to let it go, there and then, and then live with the regret, or dive into the unknown ... And perhaps be disappointed. That's real life: not an app you can open or close.'

'But with the app it's the same thing, really! You check people out as you did before across a room, except that the room is just bigger, and there is less chance of barking up the wrong tree.'

Anton pulled a face.

'I'm sceptical. I think that nothing can replace that direct experience of exchanging glances, the tingles you feel in your body when that happens.'

'No, really, the technology is just part of us now, like the bike is part of you, of these Dutch people who stay on their bikes even when they are at the cashpoint getting money. I mean, the point is not to have virtual friends. It is about the physical intensity of the encounter, the space it opens up in our life. The app is just the means of getting to that: it is a part of us now. Maybe that's something the exhibition will help you understand. There will be something about that. I think they even started to install that section already – I could take some pictures when I go back to the museum tomorrow. It's still in a chaotic phase, but I think that when the show is all up, you will see that it exactly addresses these issues. David's happy so far with the way it is turning out, by the way.'

'Well, if David is happy, I'm happy too,' he quipped. 'I am just not ready for that yet. Now let me look at your tyres. I'll put the brakes back together later.'

I took Anton's place on the steps in the lowering sun and absent-mindedly fished the phone out of my pocket while he upturned the bike and began to prod the wheels. People walked past, families on their way to the park, dog walkers. A peaceful Sunday afternoon. Victor was drawing with coloured chalk on the pavement with a younger kid who lived a few doors down. They laughed each time a dog on a leash brushed against them, sniffing at the chalk on the pavement.

I opened several apps in turn, just to be sure, but there was still no message from Efrat. I wondered how she was, how it had been, for her, to return to Israel, if she thought of me sometimes, pined for me a little, even. I had sent a couple of messages but she had warned me her phone provider might not relay them. Maybe that was her way of saying that she just wanted a clean break.

I opened and closed a few other apps. There were no

messages from anyone else, no new email. I scrolled through various newspaper apps, then back to email. I was waiting for something to happen, for a trigger of one kind or another. Anton was checking my tyre for punctures. He plunged it into a bucket of water, pressing all along the black rubber band, looking for that tiny stream of bubbles that would indicate a hole. I felt the autumn sun on my face amidst the cooling air of the afternoon, the dampness rising from the ground.

I opened the dating app. I accepted its offer to make me visible to others once again. A face I knew smiled at me, and then another. It was comforting to see those people there. I knew I would never speak to them, would never know if they had swiped right or left, or even how tall they were. I would never know what they looked like in real life, but they were there on the app still, like old acquaintances. So, I murmured, you haven't found someone yet, you have not settled. Or you are like me, never satiated, always curious about what the next encounter might bring. We were part of something undefined, but very real, of that I was certain. I pressed the tip of my finger against the screen and swiped again.

Acknowledgements

Thank you, Vicky Allan, for the trusted friendship since Psion days; for the dazzling conversations, and the writing companionship via the Edinburgh Brussels hotline. Thank you for believing in this from the start, for your care and love, always, and for this journey. Thank you for sharing your magical agent with me.

Thank you, Carrie Pilto, for the parties in Venice, the chats in Paris, the runs in Amsterdam, for your enduring faith and affection. Also in Amsterdam, I thank Rik Tuithof.

Thank you Annaïk Lou Pitteloud, Manon de Boer, Melissa Gordon, brilliant artists and very first readers, for your honesty and kindness and for all the walks in Brussels.

Thank you, Clare Alexander, my incredible agent, for setting the bar so high, and bringing sprezzatura and warmth to our exchanges, and thanks to everyone at Aitken Alexander Associates.

Thank you, Chris White, my editor at Scribner, for your brilliant insights and unfettered enthusiasm, and to Mina Asaam, for her work on the manuscript. I extend my thanks to Ian Chapman, Suzanne Baboneau and all at Simon & Schuster UK.

Thank you, Geert Lovink, for sharing stories about the Amsterdam Internet Exchange.

Lastly, thank you Camiel van Winkel, my love, for the life we have made together.